Some Girls Do

SOME GIRLS DO

Teresa McWhirter

POLESTAR
An Imprint of Raincoast Books

Polestar Books and Raincoast Books gratefully acknowledge the support of the Government of Canada through the Book Publishing Industry Development Program, the Canada Council and the Department of Canadian Heritage. We also acknowledge the assistance of the Province of British Columbia through the British Columbia Arts Council.

Edited by Lynn Henry
Interior design by Jacqueline Verkley

National Library of Canada Cataloguing in Publication Data
McWhirter, Teresa, 1971-
  Some girls do

  ISBN 1-55192-459-5

  I. Title.
PS8575.W484S65 2002   C813'.6   C2001-911677-2
PR9199.4.M28S65 2002

Library of Congress Catalogue Number: 2002102385

Polestar, An Imprint of Raincoast Books
9050 Shaughnessy Street
Vancouver, British Columbia
Canada, V6P 6E5
www.raincoast.com

At Raincoast Books we are committed to protecting the environment and to the responsible use of natural resources. We are acting on this commitment by working with suppliers and printers to phase out our use of paper produced from ancient forest. This book is one step towards that goal. It is printed on 100% ancient-forest-free paper (100% post-consumer recycled), processed chlorine- and acid-free, and supplied by New Leaf Paper. It is printed with vegetable-based inks. For further information, visit our website at www.raincoast.com. We are working with Markets Initiative (www.oldgrowthfree.com) on this project.

1 2 3 4 5 6 7 8 9 10
Printed and bound in Canada by Friesens

For anyone who ever fed me, lent me money or let me sleep on their couch—
you know who you are.

And to James Edward McWhirter,
in loving memory.

CONTENTS

THE CITY WAKES UP

Hannah's sleep is dark and slippery; blood and hard-boiled eggs. She wakes up cold when Gritboy staggers to bed and steals the covers. He looks like a giant fetus sleeping beside her and she covers his face in little bird kisses. Keep me warm, he mumbles. And she does.

Blue wakes up on her couch, fully clothed, checks for her keys and wallet. "You're a whore," she tells the purring cat as she puts a can of tuna on the floor. Her voice sounds like the back of a bar. She'll have to call Carrotgirl; she can't remember what happened the night before, but she's pretty sure it was a good time.

Carrotgirl looks through her kitchen cupboards and pretends she lives in a grocery store. It's an important day of thrift store shopping; she needs new polyester. She makes a list in crayon, gobbles breakfast chocolate and trembles on the edge of a breakdown. Her body is used to hangovers and it takes only minutes for the sugar to hit. Then she washes the smell of everyone's cigarettes out of her hair.

Jezebel wakes up to old Metallica. She lights a smoke before she gets out of bed, then drinks two cups of coffee, wearing all black, while her hair dries. The world is the same rain or shine, but she knows people look better in the dark. During the bike ride to her studio she focuses on her new painting. Jezebel thinks in red swirls, and cold cold metal.

Eli wakes up and Jezebel is the thought that breaks with the light in his coffin-like room. He rubs his goatee then his belly and goes down. Early morning woody, chub-a-dub. He hears the clatter of pizza pans below, Tom Waits crooning and the shouts of disgruntled employees. He stays in bed, lying with the light and the smell of Jezebel's hair, where it is sweet a little longer.

Em eats yogourt and smokes a cigarette, blaring funk in the background. She stands at the mirror and checks for wrinkles, desperate to put the brakes on thirty. It's Friday and all she really wants to do is get laid. Em is always waiting for something.

Jay can't remember where he left his posse of monkey men or the name of the woman beside him, and doesn't much care. He pockets a dollar on the floor, then sneaks out of the house like an early morning burglar. He begs a cigarette on the corner, then scratches his name in the bus stop, leaving marks that are easily forgotten.

Bernice wakes up alone, and she hates that.

Oliver gazes in the bathroom mirror and decides to remodel his sideburns. The night before he got drunk with a magazine editor who puked in the bathroom of a chi-chi Moroccan cafe. Today he has to make a poster, go to class, attend two meetings with three balding men holding positions he wants. He debates which pair of underwear is his sexiest. Then he slings his leather satchel over his shoulder, thinks of the ways to get ahead.

Donna is an hour late for work but hits the snooze button. She yodels in the shower, thinks of a new colour to dye her hair. She feels like an angel in maple syrup. She already has five o'clock plans: cheap beer and loud music. Make some money, have some fun. That's all she has to do.

And finally, Lily, upstairs. She wakes up during her bath with the smell of white ginger and jasmine. She puts on her magic stockings and walks to the bakery, smiling. Back home she drinks tea and peruses the cryptic crossword. Her plants twinkle and she ignores her dishes. She is older than the rest but will play outside all day in the sunshine because she knows it doesn't last. She will throw her arms around the urchins, pull each one out into the world.

It's a whole new day and anything can happen.

PART ONE

THE GIRLS

Bernice Bares All

Blue went to see her old boyfriend, Jake. There was nothing else to do and she was hungry. Blue did this every once in a while; she figured he owed her for those goddamn apple Brown Bettys she'd made during their flailing relationship. Blue had really been into Jake. He was a decent guy but couldn't get off the sauce, and the booze was starting to get him. He wrote stories about being a drunk and Blue thought they were good. She just couldn't take his hangovers. She still loved him a bit, and it was a pretty horrible feeling.

"Hey, Blue!" Jake screeched, opening the door. He called her Blue because she was always morose. He also used to say she had a long face like a horse. "How ya doin'? Ya never come and see me anymore!" Jake wore a white T-shirt covered in dried chili sauce. His hairy chicken legs stuck out of his boxers. He looked really skinny. "Come on in. We're drinking!"

Blue flopped on the couch, on top of some books and papers. She had learned never to move things. A dark-haired girl in braids sat across the room looking at the floor.

"Drink!" Jake handed Blue a Tupperware glass. "We're starting early." He hadn't shaved in at least a week. He motioned at the girl. "This is Bernice."

Bernice Delgado. Blue knew who she was. "Hello, Bernice."

Bernice looked at Blue for a long time, then finally said hello. Jake walked by and Bernice clutched him. He toppled over and fell beside her.

"Got anything to eat?" Blue asked. Jake's place was two rooms covered in beer cans and wine bottles filled with butts. She walked into the kitchen and opened the fridge: a jar of mustard and mouldy pork-fried rice in a Styrofoam container. The sink was filled with grey, slimy water. She went back to the living room.

"There's nothing to goddamn eat here!"

"Yep," Jake agreed.

Bernice picked up her wine and drained it. "Atta girl!" Jake said. Bernice had a large, pointed nose and small, blue eyes. Bernice also had enormous tits. She could've been eighteen or twenty-eight; she had the ageless look of a person unaffected by the world. Blue poured herself more wine.

"Whattya been doing?" she asked Jake.

"Drinking."

"Yeah?"

"Bernice is in nursing school."

Bernice began to rub the inside of Jake's thigh. He continued on. "I beat up a guy last night," he said. "I got kicked out of the bar."

"Why?"

"The bouncer's a dick!"

"Why'd you beat him up?"

"He was hitting on Bernice. He said he wanted to see her goodies!"

Bernice smiled vaguely. Suddenly she began to unbutton her T-shirt. She wore a stretched black bra and ripped that off, too. She got up and started to dance. Blue picked up the wine bottle. She really had something on Jake now.

"Jesus Christ, Bernice!" said Jake.

Bernice tweaked her nipples.

"What the hell?" Blue said. Bernice kept dancing. The room was very quiet. Bernice began to hum through her huge nose. She smiled and Blue stared at her bottom teeth.

"Bernice, Jesus Christ!" Jake hollered.

"Holy shit!" said Blue.

"Sorry about that." Jake went to the kitchen and got another bottle. Bernice stopped dancing and sat down on the bed. "She likes girls, too," Jake called from the other room.

"You've got a real wild one, buddy," Blue said. It was weird to talk about Bernice like she wasn't there. "Real wild fucking guacamole."

Jake and Blue settled into a fairly normal conversation about people they knew and the long-lost cat. Bernice was still motionless on the bed. Blue wondered what would happen if she stayed and they all got really loaded.

"I'm going," she said, and gathered her bag. Blue was still hungry but she knew Jake was probably broke so didn't bother nagging him for money. It bothered her, thinking about what Bernice and he would do when she left. Christ, with all the windows open.

"Sorry about Bernice," Jake said as he walked Blue to the door. She could tell he meant it.

Blue opened the door and looked back at Bernice. Then she laughed. It was an ugly sound. For a minute she felt great.

Down the hall she heard Jake yell, "Bernice, you stupid cunt!"

"I'm sorry ... I'm sorry," Bernice sobbed.

Blue slammed the exit door. Jake was turning into a real creep. She wondered if he'd always been one and she'd never noticed.

On the stairs she stopped to count her change. She had the feeling it was going to be a shitty day, and that Bernice would bother her for a long, long time.

The Lonely Dominatrix

"losin all touch, losin all touch, building a desert ..."
—some rock band

Eli saw Jezebel push through the bar with a pint in each fist and it was like the weather suddenly changed. She made him think of the beautiful, silent girls from high school who drew intricate artwork on the covers of textbooks and dated bikers on the weekend. Girls who looked like they were born bored. Jezebel's front tooth was slightly chipped, and it made Eli remember cruising cars and heavy metal, the long frustrating nights in his teenage room.

The lights in the bar flashed pink and yellow and he watched her dance. She looked tough and hard, but when she swayed her arms she seemed like a transported angel. The song ended and she walked by, swinging her long hair. "What're *you looking at*, Eli," she said. It sounded like an accusation. With Jezebel, it was hard to tell.

Eli went back to the bar every night for a week. Finally he saw Jezebel in the corner playing darts. She was wearing combat boots, black jeans and a black T-shirt with some death metal band on the front. Her shiny dark hair hung straight down her back, almost to her waist. Eli couldn't believe a girl like that would be drinking in the same bar with people like him. He watched her push some short guy with a shaved head away from her game. "Get out of my face," she told the guy. "You've already had to apologize for how you acted last week. I'm not going to give you the chance to do it again."

Eli walked over. "Need any help, Jezebel?" he asked.

"No." She turned and went to sit at her table.

Jezebel was sitting with her friend Hannah and with Oliver, an old club kid who worked at the Milk Bar. They gave each other freebies. Eli worked in a cheap pizza place and knew a lot of people.

Eli decided to sit down. "How's it going, everybody?"

"I'll tell you how it's going," Hannah said. "It's taking forever!"

"I'm not inspired," Oliver said. "I look around the city and think, where are the sexy people?" He put one hand on his hip and stuck out his chin. "WHERE ARE THE SEXY PEOPLE?"

"You've already slept with them," Jezebel said.

The band started up, some alterna-rawk ensemble in radiation suits. Groupies in baby doll dresses jerked at the edge of the stage. The lead singer had huge mutton chops. Hannah went to take a closer look.

"Hey, if any of you are going to land on the stage and knock the microphone, could you make sure my TEETH aren't against it," the singer yelled. The guitarist spat on the stage.

"This is the kind of band you have to speed up to turn off," Eli said to Jezebel. She smirked and went to play pool.

"If she's rude it usually means she likes you," Oliver said, signalling for another crantini.

The band played louder and Eli got drunker. Oliver described Jezebel's paintings. When she finally came back to the table, Oliver made a big show of going to make a phone call. Eli finished his drink. He told Jezebel he loved her.

"Mmmm-hmmm," she said.

"I'm serious." Then Eli admitted he'd always had a thing for girls with long brown hair tucked behind their ears.

Jezebel stepped away, disdainful.

"Look," Eli said seriously, "I'm almost twenty-eight. I'm only going to wait around a few years for you, tops."

When she laughed Eli thought it sounded like the first day of school, when everything is going your way.

*

It was a Sunday afternoon and it seemed like the end of the world. Jezebel twisted her long hair into a bun, which held as if by magic at the base of her neck.

"Don't *ravage* me," Oliver said. "I just asked about Eli." They sat by the window in a diner and watched the street outside. Oliver worked in a hip coffee shop and loved gossip. More importantly, he liked to be the one to tell someone else.

"Don't try to turn me into an anecdote," Jezebel warned.

She fingered the sharp points of plastic on the ripped seat until she realized what she was doing. She craned to see that her bike, with the leather saddlebags and AC/DC stickers, was still locked outside. It was a serious bike she had paid for herself. Jezebel had few possessions, but took meticulous care of each one. A deranged man in a filthy blanket walked past the window, muttering.

"Nice street," she said. A muzak version of "Let it Be" played through the restaurant.

"Murders have been planned here," Oliver whispered. It was not his kind of place; there were no cute waiters or house salads. Still, it was in Jezebel's neighbourhood and it was necessary to pick a spot where she could smoke.

They turned over their mugs and pretended not to see the light brown hair on the table, which Oliver quickly removed. Jezebel was extremely germ conscious.

They ordered coffee and nothing else. The waitress scurried away and Oliver leaned forward, shaking his creamer as if he were having an orgasm and adding it to his coffee in one giant, phallic spurt.

"I happen to know Eli likes you."

"Why, because he bought some drinks?" Jezebel narrowed her eyes and stirred her coffee slowly. "What do you know?"

Oliver looked for the waitress. He asked for more creamo. "Well, it's obvious. And Hannah had it verified from Carrotgirl." They sat silently and Jezebel smoked.

"I'm no good in relationships," she said finally. "The guys back home said I should have 'Best before two months' tattooed across my chest."

"What do you want, then?" Oliver asked impatiently. The story was going nowhere. Jezebel rolled her eyes and crushed the cigarette in the ashtray. Silver snakes twisted in a ring on her finger. She was tall and thin but her hands were strong and the canvasses she painted were nightmare swirls in green and purple, angry slashes of colour. For frames she used jagged scraps of metal she enjoyed welding together.

"I'd like to start a cult, but I hear it takes a lot of work."

"It takes a lot of work to fill your breasts with milk," Oliver replied.

"Sweet corn of Christ," she said, as Oliver tittered.

Jezebel had left the metropolis and come across the water to this island city, softly nestled between mountains and a day's drive from old growth forests. She lived in a house with a tough Chicana who studied race relations at the university and hid how the green city parks terrified her. In six months Jezebel had painted four canvasses, each of which had sold for over a thousand dollars. Her parents had no idea what she was doing with her life.

"So, what about Eli?" Oliver was determined. "Admit that you find this amusing."

They went outside and Jezebel unlocked her bike. "If you repeat this conversation to anyone, you're meat," she said as they parted ways.

Jezebel rode home, grinding the metal of her gears. It was unusually cold. Since he kept asking, she decided to meet up with Eli, at a spot of her choosing. She would figure out what kind of game he was playing. In her room she turned on the heat and stood at the window, watching car after car. The headlights cutting the dark were like ants moving through sand, and she wondered what Eli really wanted.

*

Eli found out Jezebel was having an art show and got an invitation. He went alone and stood by the bar in his clean shirt and pants. Jezebel ignored him for a while, and after a few drinks he cornered her.

"Do you have to be so aggressively indifferent to me?" he asked, and Jezebel actually laughed and touched his arm.

"I can't believe you're wearing a dress," he said.

"Don't say a goddamn word," she warned.

"What if later you have to strip down a car?"

They walked around the show and Eli told Jezebel he liked her paintings, which were admittedly disturbing. Mixed between layers of colour were images of twisted bodies, burned landscapes, exploding homes.

"Sometimes it's good to look at something beautiful," she said, "and think of the ways it will be destroyed."

Jezebel demanded a bottle from the bar and they sat alone on the terrace. She said she didn't want to be inside, forced to answer stupid questions. Eli thought she was secretly nervous to show her work; this made her easier to talk to. They agreed it was best to move on the edge of a crowd. Jezebel told Eli that she had dealt drugs as a teenager and hid tabs of acid in the elastics of her long hair. That she hated school but got straight A's in art. That as an experiment she dropped acid every day for three months to see if her eyes would bleed.

They decided to leave, and Eli said they should go to the pizza parlour; he lived upstairs. Jezebel said no, but he could walk her home. When they got to her place, Eli was surprised she invited him in, but then she wasn't comfortable and kept worrying that her roommate would come home. Eli just sat and admired her style: boots, biceps, a single bracelet. He inched closer and Jezebel moved back.

"Eli, do you understand I'm not going to get involved in anything I can't walk away from tomorrow?"

"Oh, yes," he said. "Inherently." The answer was right. Jezebel agreed he could stay, for the night.

In the morning she kicked him out early and didn't return his phone calls for three days. Then she called and said he could see her. She said he was lucky; she usually didn't even give out her phone number. Eli came right over. He brought a pizza from the restaurant and hung out while she painted. A few days later, she called him again and they did the same thing. She said she might give him a canvas for his birthday.

One night she fell asleep curled up with her back to him as he read and absently stroked her hair. Suddenly she moaned and opened her eyes. Her cheeks were flushed and a few hairs stuck to her neck with sweat.

"Eli," she said in her sleep, and his heart stopped. "Eli, I feel so good when you're here." Much later he would realize it was the only nice thing she ever said to him.

*

As a kid, Jezebel had spent nearly two years on the street, dealing. Her parents were wealthy and educated, but their money was not her money. Her father was an associate professor of literature and her mother had a master's degree in library sciences. Jezebel didn't like to read. They lived in a big house in Lonsdale and she used to imagine lighting a fire and burning it like a pile of old, dead wood.

As soon as Jezebel could, she snuck out every night. She soon learned that as long as she was clean and coherent for dinner, her mother and father didn't care what she did. Like most professional parents, they knew nothing of the secret world inhabited by their children until it cracked wide open. When she was fifteen Jezebel sat at the window and watched her older sister tear screaming from the house in her pyjamas. She ran barefoot down the street as Jezebel cheered from the window. Her father dragged her sister back with one hand clamped over her mouth. She howled between his fingers and upstairs Jezebel howled, too.

From the time she was fourteen years old Jezebel had loved a boy named Tom. Her parents saw them together once and refused to let him in their house. He was older, intense and always wired on something. Jezebel liked that he hung out in bad places, but he was also the smartest person she had ever met. His theories of light and darkness and the universe could take her on a trip for hours. Tom lived in a rat-trap downtown with his mom. Jezebel thought his mother was a real cunt; whenever she got a new boyfriend she'd kick Tom out or sign him up in a group home for crazies. And still Tom could take care of

himself, and Jezebel, too. She felt safe being Tom's girl. He had depth
when everything in her life was surface.

They were together until right before she graduated. Tom had quit
school years before. She met him outside the arcade one day. He hadn't
been around for a week or so and seemed edgy and impatient on the
phone. He said he was taking her to a special rooftop nearby. He told
Jezebel he had a present for her and they were gonna get high. She
laughed as they kept climbing. On the roof they sat and smoked. Tom
had a little stereo and they listened to music and walked back and forth
across the roof.

The sun was so hot. Everything began slowing down. Tom stood
bare-chested on the ledge, skinny arms out for balance. "Oh, I love my
Jezebellll," he sang.

"Stop it!" she yelled, and covered her eyes. "You may as well quit it
because I'm not watching you."

"JEZEBELLLL ..."

"I'm not looking!"

"Jezebel." Something was wrong and her eyes flew open. Tom
began to run as fast as he could across the ledge, like some kind of
young god with a ponytail and ripped tennis shoes. For a moment it
was gruesome and wondrous, then on the corner his foot slipped.

Jezebel's nightmares are soundless, and she's always on the roof.
The silence is worse than the screams she heard, all the way down.

*

One day Eli got a phone call from Jezebel, asking him to come over.
Recently they'd be hanging out and then she'd disappear for a few days,
turn up silent and say nothing was wrong. She got angry when he asked
her anything remotely personal. Eli followed her into the studio, where
she began mixing paints, a cigarette in her mouth like always.

"What's going on?" he asked.

"Nothing. I'm cleaning up, so don't get too comfortable. Your shit's in a bag by the door." Four CDs, a T-shirt and two pairs of socks. "You don't live here, y'know."

Eli found his carton of Marlboros in the bathroom and asked if she wanted some. When she said no, he knew something was seriously wrong. Jezebel smoked almost two packs a day. He sat on the couch and after awhile she looked up, startled.

"Christ, Eli," Jezebel said. She slashed more paint across the canvas. "Learn to contain your disease."

"So is that it? It's over?"

"Is *what* over?"

Eli walked to the door and looked back. Jezebel wasn't watching.

*

"Eli's a pod person," Jezebel stated. She had been roaming around on her bike for hours and now sat at Hannah's, smoking a roach. Hannah was one of the few people she trusted enough to get high with.

"A pod person?" Hannah asked.

"A former member of the human race whose old body has become a pod and their new body is really the organic matter of an evil alien race."

"Why do you say this?"

"Eli just doesn't understand the rules of my planet."

Hannah found this tremendously entertaining. "Nah, Eli's a narc, if anything. He's planted, man!"

"He asks too many questions."

"Poor Eli with a broken heart," Hannah said. "What do you do to these guys?"

"Say something like that again, Hannah," Jezebel said calmly, "and I'll cut your fucken throat."

*

Eli pined over Jezebel. "She's more than just another girl," he moaned to anyone who would listen. "She broke my heart."

He went out for beers one night, determined to have a good time. He lured Hannah into the alley to smoke dope and turned melancholy. Eli was used to Jezebel's sudden mood swings and unpredictable behaviours, but he had a feeling this time it was for good.

"I don't know what to say," Hannah said, squatting on her heels and looking up earnestly, "but I promise I won't tell anyone you cried."

*

A woman in a leather jacket with long hair like Jezebel's walked past the pizza pit and Eli, stacking chairs, did a double take. Gritboy, a new employee, rode in and out of the kitchen on his skateboard. "Forget it, man," he said. "Drink beer!"

"Nothing means anything without her," Eli said glumly.

Gritboy pulled his goatee. "Nothing, being nothing, makes it something."

Eli told him to take off and Gritboy rode out the parlour door, twirling an imaginary lasso in one hand and whooping.

The night janitor arrived and Eli went upstairs. His room was coffin-like, with a Union Jack that covered the tiny window and air that smelled like warm bread. He was about to go to bed when he heard a knock. The door swung open.

"Can I come in?" Jezebel asked, wiping her paint-stained hands against her shirt.

Eli swung his legs over the edge of the bed. "You think you can just dump me and then come over and everything's okay?" He held out his arm. "Well, it is."

Jezebel smiled weakly and sat on the edge of the bed.

"I'm so tired," she said. Eli moved to stroke her hair. Jezebel stayed in the same position, but pushed his arm away.

"Don't," she said.

Carrotgirl on Her Bike

Carrotgirl called Blue early and said to come right over. Today was the day she had to go see her ma, and last night she had tied one on to get ready.

Blue walked into Carrotgirl's apartment and wasn't surprised to see the bed already made. They used to live together with a drunk named Gritboy above a Chinese grocery, and Blue knew Carrotgirl didn't wake up like other people, whether she'd been drinking or not. She leapt out of bed with a horrible grin on her face and started to clean, even if she was still drunk. Carrotgirl was terrifyingly clean, and the nicest girl Blue had ever met. She didn't just give away her spare change, she took her favourite bums for picnics in the park. If she had a hangover, then after her chores she rode her bicycle on all-day missions of goodwill and penance. Sometimes she made muffins.

Blue found Carrotgirl in the kitchen, meticulously aligning the rugs to the tiled floor. "I've been busy," she said standing up. "I been talking to other worlds." Her home was colourful and, of course, immaculate. Porcelain carrots hung from the ceiling by invisible thread and Formica turnips sat polished in a painted bowl. Blue missed living with Carrotgirl. She had left town to travel to Australia, following a boy now simply referred to as Ratbag.

Carrotgirl wore a frilly flowered apron and wielded an enormous feather duster. She liked to dress for any occasion. She began to polish the framed Winnie the Pooh pictures and photos of Prince Harry. Carrotgirl had a real thing for Prince Harry, the little one. She said she'd like to grab hold of those big, pink ears.

"Did you get in trouble last night?"

"Oh, I'm going to heaven," Carrotgirl said, "but first I'm gonna burn for my sins in the suburbs. Down down down down down down YEEHA!" She opened the fridge and put her mouth underneath the gala keg of wine on the top shelf. She steadied herself and opened the spout. "AAAAHHHH!" she gargled.

Carrotgirl loved to drink. It didn't matter what: cheap beer, red wine, sambuca (black or white), rye, scotch, gin, vodka, ouzo, tequila, cider, schnapps, moonshine. She lived for a bender. She expressed a deep love for elephants, pink pigs and cats. Eventually this turned lecherous, Carrotgirl with her famous foul mouth and backlog of dick jokes. When they ran out of alcohol, Carrotgirl devised impossibly intricate schemes to find more, and if she didn't, sweet jeez she was like a freckled powerhouse on a course of rampant destruction. She lined her bike basket with flowers and smelled like strawberries, but once she'd punched a guy outside a liquor store and he stayed down. She enthusiastically threw shot glasses over her shoulder. The week before she had driven her bike down the apartment hallways at midnight, roaring camp songs.

Carrotgirl's apartment was mostly pink. She had a rotary phone that was impractical but pink, too. The phone was part of a property war with Carrotgirl's ex-roommate, Donna Delgado, who still hadn't paid the bill. Donna still came around. She said her new roommate didn't like to go slumming. Donna had just got a job in the mall, but she used to be on welfare, just like Carrotgirl and Blue.

Carrotgirl offered Blue a muffin and danced with the Tupperware container. Carrotgirl had pale skin, black bobbed hair and blue eyes, and Blue thought she looked like Snow White, but twisted, 'cause she was covered in head to toe freckles and had a huge, gap-toothed smile. It was hard to believe the sweetness hadn't got beaten out of her, all things considered.

Carrotgirl still talked about how one day she and her dad would live in a little cottage together, a cottage with a garden. He'd gone to prison when she was little for getting high and crazy and shooting up the house. Carrotgirl and her brother had been hiding upstairs and the bullets that went through the floor barely missed them. Her mom phoned the police and Carrotgirl wasn't even allowed to say goodbye. They were a weird, poor family who lived on a farm. The police found a grow operation and lots of coke and some guns. Her dad used to be a biker, she said, and was pretty fucken cool. After he left they had to move into town. Carrotgirl's mom was a waitress and worked nights at the Legion, where Blue had met her once. It was a scary place. Her mom was an old alcoholic and kind of puffy, but Blue could tell she used to be really beautiful. She had blue eyes that squeezed dollars out of bar drunks.

"You're gonna come with me, right? To my mom's? Please? She won't leave me alone about the Bob job! Will you come with me? Please? Okay?"

Bob was Carrotgirl's mother's bowling partner. Her mother was determined to get Carrotgirl a job at his doughnut shop. Carrotgirl used to babysit for Bob. One day he had tried to feel her up in the kitchen, and no adults had believed her when she ratted on him.

Carrotgirl had been told by her mother to dress nicely for the interview, so she sported an enormous black hat completely covered in white daisies that looked like the top of a hair dryer you sit under at a beauty salon.

"That hat is bizarre," Blue said, with wonder.

Carrotgirl admitted she'd had to try on three different outfits until she found the right one. "Whee," she sang. "*Bahbra-Ann*, hair of traaans-aaam." Carrotgirl jerked around the kitchen like a crazy person. "Afterwards we'll grab the box of wine from the fridge and go sit in the park." She did the knee-hand shuffle, yelling "Hoo-HA, hoo-HA!" Blue told her she sounded like an old Jewish lounge singer and they thought that was pretty funny.

They went downstairs and Carrotgirl unlocked her bike. "Hop on," she said, "we're gonna seat ride."

Blue loved it when Carrotgirl doubled her. She had a big red Raleigh and Blue sat on the rat trap. Carrotgirl pedalled fast down the crowded streets, dodging between buses, right past a big-bellied traffic cop.

"Heeey piggy," she squealed and shook the plastic fish mounted on her bike basket. "El Bandito!" she hollered. "Whee!"

They rode up and down the streets, past three-storey homes with well-tended gardens. Carrotgirl was skinny and wiry and really strong. She slowed down on the uphills but they made it no problem. The houses in the neighbourhood looked so nice they didn't seem real.

"Hello! Hi there!" Carrotgirl waved to an old man outside his Victorian home. He stared back over the hedges, unsmiling. "Well!" Carrotgirl said, "I never!" Blue gave him the finger and they continued on.

They rode past the hospital and a cluster of Asian groceries, into unimaginative housing units, convenience stores, strip malls. Beyond this, things broke down. Dilapidated homes and potholes. Carrotgirl pointed out backyard chop shops. They saw walls of graffiti and tried to figure out the tags. There was a huge mural of the moon and aliens in an empty lot. "Why don't they turn these into city gardens to feed all the hungry people?" Carrotgirl asked. Blue didn't even answer.

Carrotgirl rode past her mom's house and parked down the block. They crept up the street into the yard like home invaders. Carrotgirl was skilled in this and other methods of petty crime. A recycling box filled with yellow newspapers and sour milk bottles sat on the porch beside an old couch that rotted wetly. The place was a dump and Blue felt bad for Carrotgirl. She couldn't imagine calling a place like this home.

"Get down," Carrotgirl hissed, and they ducked beneath the kitchen window. She pulled out a pair of enormous black sunglasses from her bag and Blue snorted into her hand. Then they peeked in the window. Carrotgirl's mother sat at the table in her waitress uniform. Her blonde hair had inch-long roots, and for some reason Blue was sure her hands smelled like onions. They peeked again. A deck of cards lay scattered over the table. A coffee cup read, "If You Think Sex is a Pain in the Ass You're Doing It Wrong" above a cartoon donkey in a straw hat. They could smell dishes of old food in the sink.

"UhwaHHH, UHwaHHH, UHwaHH!" cried baby Dylan, Carrotgirl's nephew. Carrotgirl's mother slammed down her cup and stormed across the kitchen. Blue used to have a crush on Carrotgirl's brother, Lettuce. He got that name because he got scurvy after eating nothing but cheese pizza and beer for six months. It was the only reported case in the province in the last one hundred years. He got kind of famous for it. Carrotgirl said it wasn't funny, his gums were cracked and bleeding and he was sick for a long time. Lettuce was in jail for fraud, and Dylan was the product of a conjugal visit. Carrotgirl said there was a trailer right there on the prison grounds. Janice, her brother's girlfriend, had six toes on one foot. Sometimes Janice threatened to kill herself and the baby.

Carrotgirl's ma came back, trying to juggle the baby and light a cigarette. Dylan's skin was the colour of yellow milk and there was a rash of white bumps across his cheeks. It didn't seem possible, but he screamed even louder.

Carrotgirl crept off the steps and waved for Blue to follow. "GADDAMN IT," they heard her ma yell, "GADDAMMIT YOU STOP THAT!" They walked down the block and Carrotgirl pushed her bike.

"I could put that baby out of his misery," Carrotgirl said.

They walked on and Blue kept quiet. "I could do it," Carrotgirl said again.

"Whoa," Blue said. At the top of a huge hill Carrotgirl told her to hop on and they pushed off.

Carrotgirl began to pedal. Houses sped by in a blur and she crouched over the handlebars. She pedalled faster and faster. Halfway down the hill Carrotgirl began to scream, "HEY MISTAH, MISTAH BA-NA-NA, TAKE ME TO DA COPA-CABANA!" Blue let go of her knapsack and wrapped her arms around Carrotgirl's waist. They were going so fast it didn't seem like they'd be able to stop.

The Last Dogman

Em was a beautiful, unhappy girl. She woke up depressed (again!) for no real reason. She stared at herself naked in the full-length mirror and then decided to go to the gym. After lifting weights she wanted a soak but there were men in the hot tub with moustaches so she went shopping instead. She stole a pair of jeans from a thrift store, but not even petty theft made her feel better. At home she heard Hannah and Jezebel laughing next door and reached for the phone.

"Come over," she said when Hannah answered.

"You come over *here*."

"I'm always stepping on stuff at your place."

Hannah hung up the phone. "*One* fishhook and I never hear the end of it."

"Let me guess. Em's depressed and wants company?" Hannah nodded and Jezebel rolled her eyes. "I wonder who shit in her cornflakes today?" At Em's, the three of them sat slumped on the couch and she tried to convince them to go out.

"It's Tuesday," she said. "We *always* go out and dance on *Tuesday*." Jezebel was tired and Hannah had no money, as usual. "*Okay*," Em said, "we can drink my wine." She kept a bottle in her cupboard for occasions that never seemed to come.

She sent Hannah to knock on apartment doors for a corkscrew and changed her shirt three times. She threw her new lipstick across the bathroom. "Horrible colour!" she screeched. Hannah convinced her to smoke a joint and then they went around the corner to their old bar that had reopened as a dance club with the detestable name Kooly Shakers. Em and Hannah didn't want to give up the convenience of a club next door, but Jezebel lived across town and didn't care if they had to go farther away.

"This place embodies everything I despise about corporate-sponsored nightlife," she said as they walked up the stairs. "With a god-damn *line-up*," she added.

"We had so much fun here," Hannah said sadly. They found a seat and ordered a round of drinks. Dance music flooded the room and Jezebel grimaced. Homeboys in track suits hustled poorly cut drugs.

A few drinks later the night started to pass and Em went out the back entrance to the quietly endorsed pot-smoking area that had luck-ily survived the changeover. It was empty except for a group of puffed-up jocks sharing a fifth of whisky and promising to drink themselves bloody. Back inside, Em followed an overweight woman to the bath-room and listened as she drunkenly talked about her lost youth. An angry-looking girl ignored them both and carved a name into the wall beside the sink.

Hannah and Jezebel had moved to the upper couches. They pointed to Bernice and laughed as she danced in a short, sequined top. "Watch, soon that girl will be waving her ass in the air," Jezebel pre-dicted. Hannah agreed subtlety was not an option for those unable to make their own lunch. Em told them to come and dance and they laughed like drunken hyenas.

Em stood on the corner of the floor and felt the same loneliness she did in the bathtub, with nothing to occupy her mind but the ceiling. The boy beside her said hi and Em straightened up. She had seen him dance and liked the devilish look under his ball cap, a smile like he had a joke no one knew. He bought her a beer and said his name was Jay and that he'd noticed her before, which was true because Em had long, lovely limbs that stretched like a cat's. They danced and talked and got drunk, and she was amazed he stayed by her side all night. As it neared closing time, Em told herself to be bold and said, "I live around the corner. Do you want to come over?" Jay said he did and Em was a little surprised, even though she'd seen the situation before and didn't have to doubt his signals.

They agreed to meet back at the door. Em found Hannah and Jezebel and pointed out the boy she was taking home. "So *that's* where you've been," Hannah whistled and slapped her hand, but Jezebel shook her head.

"I've seen him around before. Watch out for that one," she warned.

Hannah yelled that the night was young and cute boys would always be cute boys.

Jezebel argued that men were the downfall of great female artists. "Like Camille Claudel."

Hannah couldn't resist. "Elizabeth Smart!"

Jezebel knew Em had survived early puberty and small town cocaine and didn't understand why she wasn't smarter about men. But Hannah knew it was hard to believe good things about yourself until someone else said them first. They watched Jay and Em walk out with his arm around her. "It'll end up bad," Jezebel said. "She doesn't understand that you can use them right back."

"A hump, a dump, then a big blonde grump," Hannah said. They agreed they'd seen that one before.

*

In Em's apartment, Jay tried to kiss her at the window. "Hey, I like you," he said.

Em said, "Really?"

Jay lit her cigarette and said, "Yeah."

Em searched for rolling papers and accidentally sat on top of the cat in the bean bag chair. When Jay laughed she realized he was appealing on the base level that affected all women: in certain moments he looked like a little boy.

Act like you're fourteen years old
everything you say is so obnoxious funny true and mean
I'd love to be your blowjob queen

The stereo played Liz Phair and they passed the joint. Em

explained the psychedelic art over her bed while Jay pawed through the dish of blue rocks from the beach. Outside they heard the club begin to shut down: cars honking and groups of drunken men who stood in the road, bellowing. Jay told Em he'd had a crush on her for a long time. She thought it could be true; the city they lived in was small. He asked if she had a boyfriend and when Em said no, Jay grabbed her hand and said, "*You're beautiful,*" and for once Em thought, *Yeah.*

Em decided to give in and gave it up and got naked and dirty and she and Jay made each other feel really good. Later they sat in a tub filled with bubbles and Jay wrapped his arms around her. "I can't believe I found a girl like you." Em was amazed that two people could feel so alive right there in the heart of the city.

*

The next day Em called Hannah and said, "We went out for coffee this morning and then we were walking down the street and he saw a bunch of his friends and he gave me a big hug like he wasn't ashamed of being with me."

Hannah said, "Wow! He sounds great!"

Em invited Jay over for dinner that night and went to the Italian deli and talked about cheeses, bought fresh lasagna noodles and focaccia bread, wine and flowers at the corner grocery. She put her sheets in the laundry, lit incense and cleaned the tub. To pass time she had a bath and thought of Jay and how lucky she was, and she smelled the lasagna cooking and wondered if after dinner he'd want to go to a movie and if he would hold her hand. She put on perfume and only began to worry when Jay was an hour late. Two hours passed and the salad withered. When the lasagna dried out Em knew he wasn't coming. She phoned Hannah, who came right over.

"The dogman didn't even *call?*" she said, and Em started to cry.

They went upstairs to see Lily, who was older and together and by far the wisest girl they knew. Hannah pulled out a joint from her cigarette pack and Lily made tea while Em told the story, how after all Jay said she thought he really liked her, that they were starting a relationship.

"*I don't understand!*" Em sniffed. "He said he couldn't believe he'd found me!"

Barf, Hannah thought.

"Sometimes we force an intimacy that isn't there," Lily said gently when Em wouldn't stop crying.

"I just want those romantic cliches," Em wailed.

"Why?" Lily finally asked. Em was at the window, not listening. She saw a shadow on the street and thought it might be him.

Lily & the Devil

Lily rushed down the stairs, silver hearts and chains swinging from her neck. Even Em stopped scowling when Lily was around.

"How was work?" Em asked.

"Office girls, office girls, wanna be dumb, RICH girls," Lily sang on the corner as they waited for the light to change. She'd had a relaxing weekend of munching pot cookies (made with green butter) and reading her tarot. At the security building where she worked she had moved two lounge chairs in front of her computer terminal and reclined until horizontal to her keyboard. When her supervisor had raised an eyebrow and asked if she could be any more comfortable, Lily had closed her eyes and thought of her lovely bed. Lily said there were too many things in the world she wanted to try, and she never stayed in one job for long.

"Do you feel better about this Jay fellow?" Lily asked. "How *is* he?"

"He's a fool. He could have been with *me!*"

Lily clapped her hands. "Precisely."

Em and Lily lived in the same building, along with Carrotgirl and Hannah, but Lily's apartment was a refuge. She kept a windowsill garden of herbs and mixed tinctures that cured any ailment. The kitchen table at the window held flowers, painted teapots and an intricate box filled with charms. In the living room there was polished wood, African masks, pillows piled on a thick red carpet. In the middle of the room stood an old brass bed with a homemade quilt so old no one could trace the bloodstains. She had stacks and stacks of books she would consult or pass along: dictionaries of dreams, books on giants, sunflowers, dead celebrities. She strung loose beads on twists of silver for bookmarks and turned brown with the slightest bit of sun. She stayed naked all summer. Lily had the wisdom of gypsies.

Sometimes Em came over to drink coffee in the morning and Lily told her stories. About working on a pot farm, learning to play bass from the musician who still wrote her songs. About the white sand beaches of Mozambique. That she talked too much to the animals, detested the Catholic church and enjoyed the sound of smashing glass.

Lily was leaving the city when the summer ended, going back East to sell her jewellery. She lived by a sliding scale but would take big bucks from city folk who asked if she had something quaint yet funky for a gala opening. Em, too, talked of leaving the grim city glimmer. She wanted to see other countries, but loathed airplanes, buses and trains.

They were headed to the Dirty Dollar for cheap draft. On the corner they stopped to look at a moon that was bigger than they had ever seen. They smoked a joint, rolled Drum and wished for a grapefruit while watching the whores glide past with their steel calves and dull lips.

The bouncer ignored the crowd at the door but lifted the velvet rope and greeted Lily. She always said hello and chatted when she passed him standing outside the club, watching for trouble to come in or out. Inside, Lily and Em waited beside a group of young men in expensive pre-washed jeans, shirts sporting corporate logos. "This isn't a queer bar, is it?" one of them asked. They regarded Lily in her travelling pants, swinging a purse like a medicine bag, and molested her with their horrible fish stares. "Yeeeah," they bellowed, "Yeaaah!"

Lily leveled her finger like a gun and pointed at each of their faces and BOOM! BOOM! BOOM!

"You're dead," she said, "I erased you."

Em kept close to Lily, drawing on her sparkles. The bartender, notorious Andrew, lazily scratched one freckled arm tattooed in black water creatures. "What?" he snarled, and when Lily smiled warmly he looked visibly confused. The speaker featured an enormous dancing dyke with leather titty straps. It took a moment to adjust to the thrum of energy, the darkness and searching eyes.

Many years before, the Dirty Dollar had been a hardcore club, and the spray-painted walls could be seen faintly through new coats of peeling paint. Jerry, the greasy owner, had implemented these changes in decor after raising the price of beer by a dollar. He owned a mansion in the hills and made his wife, a hot Asian tart, work the coat check. The bar was a crumbling monolith, a monument to a private world before grunge hit the runways. It made the old-timers sad and wistful, for reasons not quite remembered.

Punks in hoods and camouflage gear joined forces with rockers in layers of sour-smelling hair to fight for space against pseudo-hipsters in clean shirts. Girls with unobtrusive nose studs were eyed suspiciously by spandex sluts with dagger nails and stiletto boots. The music — angry, snarling guitar, heavy, thumping bass and shouted atrocities — combined with an unusually small dance floor, enhanced the combative nature of the club. Either they danced like they'd seen it all before and it bored them to nausea or they moved in step, following unfathomable leads, caught in the spirit of a slaughterhouse herd.

Lily came because she found energy, expressed in any form, highly invigorating. People thought her the strangest of all because she walked around smiling.

Em looked around with distaste. "Why are we here, Lily?"

"Think of yourself as Columbus," she said, then reconsidered. "Without an agenda."

Lily found many spooks out to play. Hannah, the downstairs dealer and favourite elf, danced like she was holding a wheelbarrow; Jezebel, her bodyguard, in an Iron Maiden T-shirt and leather jacket; Carrotgirl and Blue plowing through the crowd with Heineken labels stuck to their foreheads.

Time slipped away like an acid trip as the music rumbled and farm boys clenched their fists.

A song began and a pair of skinny, shy girls dancing together looked around frantically as the floor emptied and everyone sneered at the song. People began to snicker as they stayed on the dance floor, shuffling alone in embarrassment.

"Why is no one dancing?" Lily asked. "This song sounds the same as the last one." She strutted out onto the dance floor and joined the girls, who smiled gratefully and began to move their feet faster.

Then out boogied the devil.

The song changed and everyone rushed to be near him. One of the shy girls waited in the corner while her friend went to the bathroom. She was hot and uncomfortable and wanted to go home. The devil suddenly stood in front of her. "Janelle O'Dell, you have a genius IQ," he said as her mouth fell open. "Don't try to mix with the animals."

The devil was the subject of a distinct urban bullshit mythology: he dosed every night; he kept a dominatrix; he'd stabbed a guy in a bar fight. He was a model, a junkie, the son of the singer of a cult band known for molesting groupies.

"YOU PUSHY PEOPLE!" the waiter screamed, and nearly bumped the devil's table. The devil let it slide. It would be the waiter's last shift; later that night in the mausoleum-like warehouse the waiter shared with a goth hairdresser he would stumble into one of the huge cement poles in the center of the room, knocking himself into a coma from which he would never awaken.

The devil could play fine zydeco music and a mean fiddle, just like in the song. He was the first and most obscene bartender to work at the Dirty Dollar. He carried his reputation like a lifeless star.

Lily made her own dance space in the corner and the devil moved next to her. He couldn't remember the last time he had been afraid; the feeling was unfamiliar and exhilarating.

"Oh, Lily," the devil said when he saw her little pink tongue.

Everyone got drunk and danced madly. Hannah pushed a midget woman in the mosh pit, something she felt bad about later. Carrotgirl threw up in the DJ booth. When the last song ended and the lights came on everyone hid their faces and looked for shadows. Motorcycle cops cruised past the crowd that pushed out of the Dirty Dollar; alliances were formed, acquaintances struck and severed, and much coffee consumed to stay awake until the sun descended on the weary city.

Lily and Em sat on the corner stoop. Jezebel remained for one last cigarette, watching a group of drunken French hippies clash with a surly group of New Democrats who had failed terribly in a dart tournament at a local Irish pub. After much boasting and threats, a head smashed against the face of a bellowing Québécois and everyone scattered.

"Check it out!" hollered Jezebel.

"Why would anyone," Lily asked in amazement, "work so hard at having a problem?"

A drunken man in skin-tight jeans staggered over. "Hello, ladies," he slurred, "you are looking for some action?"

"Oh fuck *off*," Em said.

His face turned red and he thrust his crotch angrily. "Bitches," he sneered. "White lesbians!"

"Why don't you kill yourself?" said the devil quietly from the shadows.

"Eh? What's that?"

The devil moved closer and opened his arms.

"Aieeee!" The drunken man fled screaming down the street to join his friends at the 7-Eleven and wreak havoc on rows of stale pastries.

"That was great," Lily said, retying her braid. "I just was going to say, 'Honey, take yourself home to bed.' He wasn't really having fun, was he?"

The devil and Lily eyed each other. "That was a favour," he said nervously. "Of free will."

"Give me a break," said Em, flicking her cigarette. She was secretly embarrassed; one night she had cornered the devil and told him he was beautiful. "You don't even know me," he had said with contempt, and it was so simple Em had turned away shamed and never talked to him again.

"The devil turned and disappeared," Jezebel said.

"I know who *you* are," the devil said.

"You look cold," said Lily, "sit down." The devil stood uncertainly. Lily smiled and he cupped a hand against the collar of his leather jacket and lit a thin black cigar. He felt a challenge of sorts and every-one knew the devil liked a good fight.

His eyes looked like shifting pools of mercury. Em and Jezebel said good night. "You know how much I hate people?" the devil said. "I don't even have a phone."

Lily held his hand as the crowd began to disperse. The devil felt his stomach churn at the sickening, timid drunks. He saw their cancers and decay. "Lily," he said, "please."

There was a fine line being balanced in the universe. Time ceased to exist. Lily began to walk home and the devil followed. Buddha, he remembered, felt the pain of everyone.

*

The devil sat in Lily's apartment, shuddering at the colour and com-fortable surfaces. "Do you have anything to drink?" he asked. "I need ... a drink."

"No," Lily said.

They remained still for a long time. "Do you know why the angels were kicked out of heaven, Lily?" the devil asked. "Because they chose to love themselves more than God." Then the devil pulled up his shirt, showing burns, some old and some fresh. They dotted his ribcage like the map of an ancient constellation. He dragged on his cigarette, hard. "Burn me," he said, holding it out. "Do it."

She took his face in her palms, kissed his forehead, his chin, each eyelid. "I forgive you," she said.

After Lily fell asleep, tangled in the sheets, her chest rising gently with each breath, the devil wept for all the lost time.

Girls

The morning after was marked by puke in the hallway, Mexican beer hangovers, the sour taste of tequila shots, and the end of Donna's friendship with Em.

*

The night had begun as it usually did, the girls meeting up and drinking before going out. Em wanted everyone at her place, though she then complained of the cigarette smoke and dirty glasses.

Hannah came in with Jezebel. Donna also arrived, though no one had invited her. "Should I wear these?" she asked, parading across the room in her gumboots. Donna was a big-boned girl with curves that strained at her clothing. Her brown teeth gave her a trashy look that worked with her vividly dyed clothing, but her pink hair made her round head look like a washed-out Easter egg.

"You ate all the peanut brittle, Hannah." Em shook the empty candy dish. "I thought you didn't even like it."

"I don't."

"I admire that," Jezebel said. "You're the ultimate hedonist." She crossed her legs in a way that was elegant and vaguely threatening. "Em, you're a twenty-seven year old who has shit her pants on ecstasy. Who are you to talk about anything?"

Em stomped across the room. "Hannah, quit picking at the rug."

"STOP TERRORIZING ME!" Hannah bellowed from the floor. "Please?"

"That man at the fruit stand is so cooool," Donna said, opening the curtains wider. "You have such a super view."

"Huh?"

Suddenly Donna spotted Eli coming up the street. "Hey, hot pants!" she yelled. Everyone came to the window.

"WHEREYA GOIN', ELI?"

He looked up and laughed. "Getting a haircut," he called, rubbing his head and walking. "Hi, Jezebel," he waved. She tossed her hair and put her head back in the window.

"You were a Q-tip," Hannah called down. "Now you're a Q-tip with a cotton ball on the end!"

"What are you guys doing tonight?"

"We're going to the Dirty Dollar!" Hannah yelled. Jezebel hissed and yanked her back through the window by her belt loop. "Aagghhh!"

Hannah convinced Em to smoke some weed. Jezebel wouldn't get high if she was going out and Donna never did drugs, aside from occasional psychedelic trips with weird art boys. She told them about her weekend on a small island up the coast in a hippie house where everyone tended to a huge vat of salty mushroom tea.

"If you pick up another case of scabies you're not allowed over," Em warned. "I mean it, Donna, I'm sick of it. You and your sister, I swear ..."

"*Half*-sister," Donna said loudly and shot a mean look at Em, who shrugged. "And I can't stand Bernice."

"Who can?" Em picked up her glass. "Let's get drinking," she said. "When the hell are we leaving?"

Donna began work on a secret blender drink in the kitchen. "So I like to kiss boys," she said to Hannah, who burned her hair trying to light a cigarette from the gas stove. "I don't do anything, I just kiss them. Big *deal*."

"You're a kissing bandit," Hannah agreed. Jezebel stared down the cat when she thought no one was watching, and Em bitched about her ass in the bathroom. Hannah kept sniffing her burnt hair. She was warned of the crumpled bills about to fall out of her pocket.

"Are you going to the *gathering* later?" Jezebel asked Em sarcastically. She slipped her snake ring on her first finger and grabbed at the wine. Em was older, worked a gruelling job in an art gallery that paid real cash, and liked to spend it on her own good time.

"'You're an old cougar," Jezebel said. "All you go out looking for are cute young boys."

"Impossible! There are no cute boys in this city!" said Em.

"What about Sunshine Boy?" asked Hannah.

"Who?" asked Jezebel.

"He makes all those lowriders," Em continued. "I think he's a bike courier."

Donna came out of the kitchen. Hannah took a sip of her white frothy drink and gagged. "They're all bike couriers," she said, "to some degree."

They drank more, did a final check, then found their keys and headed for the door. Since they lived downtown, everything was within walking distance. The bar already had a line-up. "I'm not going to be stuck standing at the back," Em warned.

"Hiiiiii," they leered at the bouncer. He lifted the red velvet rope and Donna swung her hips inside.

"I fucking HATE this place," Em said and smacked her palm on her forehead. "I forget and keep coming back." The bouncer overheard and nodded.

Donna made a beeline for the perfect table on the upper level. Em stayed behind to score some ecstasy. A girl walked past in a silver bra. "That's my ex-girlfriend," the bouncer said. "Can you fucking believe it?"

Em stuck a smile on her face.

"I *know* those guys," Donna said to Hannah, gesturing to three boys slouching in the corner by the DJ booth. "They went to my *high* school. They're total *poseurs*."

Hannah liked how Donna put a French spin on everything, even though she came from a poor and dysfunctional bingo family. "Really? You used to be able to tell by looking at the shoes."

"You can't do that anymore," said Donna. "They have adopted a look but not the ideology."

"That's brilliant!"

"Besides," she said, "those jeans are *way* too tight."

The bar began to fill up. Donna went to the back and watched a boy play a video game.

"Hi, Don."

"What?"

"Hi, Don."

"Don? I'm not Don."

"You're not? Are you sure?"

"Yeah."

"I thought you were somebody I know."

"Yeah, Don. I'm not Don, but I may have been in another life."

"So you're not Don. Now I feel like a loser."

"I'm Shane."

"Hiiiii," Donna said, taking his free hand.

"Oh, my hand is all sweaty."

"It's what?"

"Sweaty."

"Oh."

Em and Hannah watched a gorgeous boy walk slowly through the bar. "I can't stand that Tapeworm Boy," Em finally said.

"I think he's beautiful, like one of those statues from ancient Greece," Hannah said.

"Oh, *those*."

"I'm going to write a poem about this place," Hannah said. "It will be a tale by a turnip, signifying titty-caca."

Em and Hannah would never admit it, but each believed in true love at first sight. Even though it had never happened to them. Or anyone they knew.

"*Look* at those little chiclet girls," Em seethed. "*Look* at that girl with stickers on her face."

Hannah twisted in her seat. "Y'know, I'm down for that kinderwhore look. It really subverts the idea of girls being powerless."

"No, it means that for them I'm menopausal."

Jezebel came back from the pool table and she and Em went to the tiny bathroom. In the line a girl pulled out a bottle of hairspray from her purse. "Do you mind?" Jezebel said. "I'm just here to piss."

The girl studied her reflection in one of the mirrors. "How am I going to pick up someone with no face powder?" she wailed.

Em wanted to dance but hated the music. Jezebel would only commit to songs she already knew. Hannah had to be drunk and pried onto the dance floor by Donna, who, it could honestly be said, danced like a spastic and had the best time. Hours reeled past. A moment of significant eye contact was like a prearranged marriage.

Em staggered to the back. "Hey hotstuff!" she heard, and spotted Jay. She went over to his table and gave him the finger.

"*You* are an asshole," she said. "Thanks for standing me up."

"No baby, no," he said, taking her hand. "I had to work late that night and I lost your number."

"Sure you did."

"Yeah, and then I came by later and you weren't there."

She checked out his friends who were sitting in a vacant herd around him. "Well, I did go to Lily's to smoke a joint but only for —"

"See?" Jay said, and pulled her onto his lap. He had recently bleached his hair and Em thought he looked even cuter. "I want you to sit on my kitchen table," he told her.

"You're gross," she said, taking a cigarette. "I think I'm wasted."

"Want a drink?" Jay asked, handing over his beer. Em gulped it down and felt his hand on her stomach. She got up to leave and Jay pulled her down. "ooohh, don't go," he pleaded, licking her ear. "Whereya goin'?" Em turned and they started kissing. Then she pulled away and realized it was just Jay and his slippery charm, copping a feel at a back table.

"I've got to get *out* of here," Em said, scrambling away. "What the hell am I *doing*?" His friends watched her leave.

"Should've gotten her some gin, man."

"Panty remover," Jay agreed.

Em decided she was leaving for the rave. She got her jacket without saying goodbye. As she walked down the street, she tried to remember the doorman's name; she'd try to cut a deal so she wouldn't have to pay.

*

Hannah danced with her back to the tables that circled the floor. She hated people watching her. A sweaty boy in a buttoned-up shirt reached over and grabbed her arm. "You wanna dance?" he asked.

"I am! Dancing!" she yelled, shaking her wrists in his face. She lost her rhythm and went back to the table. "What a bunch of fuckwads," she said to no one in particular and grabbed a random beer. Eli came by and tapped her on the shoulder.

"Hey sister!" he said as they slapped palms.

"It's good to *see* you!" Hannah said. "We haven't hung out since you and Jezebel ..."

"So, is she here? Who's she with now?"

"Hey, am I still gonna get free pizza?" Hannah asked.

Eli leaned over and kissed Hannah's cheek just as Jezebel slid onto a chair.

"Every time I come here, I see you," Eli said.

Jezebel blew smoke in his face. "Maybe it's because you're looking for me."

"*Ouch!*" Eli moaned and clutched his chest.

"Don't worry about it," Hannah slurred and shoved a beer toward him. "Drink."

Jezebel left the table and came back with a shot of sambuca for Hannah. "Did mine at the bar," she said, looking at Eli. "You still here?"

Hannah gulped and felt black licorice burn a path to her belly. Eli left without a word.

"What a git," said Jezebel.

"Why don't you try dealing with your carnage sometime?" Hannah said. "Eli did used to be my friend, you know."

The truth was, sometimes Jezebel let Eli come over and brush her hair while she curled on the couch. She didn't tell her friends, but they would have understood. Loneliness was just a feeling of space, and it could be filled with so many things.

Donna took over an empty seat. "Look who I found!" she trilled.

"Who cares?" Jezebel said and bolted from the table with her jacket.
Jay sat down glumly. Hannah stormed off in the other direction.

"What's up with *those* guys?" Donna asked.

Jay picked up her hand and licked her palm. "Come over to my
place. You can make a Plasticine dinosaur."

"I might stay over at Hannah's."

"Four-star lesbians!" he cried.

"Wrong."

"Let's party!"

Donna considered his offer and hit the dance floor instead. She
relayed the story to Hannah over the music.

"As far as I'm concerned, Jay's a hick with a dye job," Hannah
hollered.

"Oh my god," Donna yelled, "you think I don't know?"

They danced until the last song. "Ugly lights!" they screamed, and
headed to the door as fast as they could.

Outside they talked about what to do. "It'll take forever for Jezebel
to cool off," Hannah said to Donna. "Did you still wanna sleep over?"

They took the hidden key and broke into Em's to get the rest of the
liquor. "I think you need to smoke weed," Hannah told Donna as they
finished drinking the last of the booze. Donna said she couldn't. "Why
not?" Hannah said. "IT'S AMMONIA-FREE!" Then she passed right out in
her chair.

*

Sometime after noon Em gave a groan, her face grey. She remembered
her shitty night and got angry all over again.

Next door, Donna grumbled from her lump on the couch. "It's
raining."

Hannah howled and drummed her legs against the mattress.
"NOOO!" They had planned on a trip to the beach to work on the pre-
dicted hangovers. Hannah wondered out loud when a pattern of

disappointment actually became a lifestyle, and Donna said she'd take her for breakfast. They heard a knock on the door and Hannah fought to free herself from the tangle of blankets. Her dreads stuck up straight in a fuzzy lump from her head. She made a face at Donna when they heard Em's voice.

"You guys look niiiice," Em said sarcastically, coming in.

"Water," Donna croaked.

"Are you guys going for breakfast? I wanna come, too."

Hannah pressed her forehead and moaned. When they were finally ready they clomped down the street to the nearest diner. They passed the bar. The only trace of the previous night was smashed green glass by the front door.

"You took off without even saying goodbye last night," Hannah said. "I'll bet you were one of those girls in high school who dumped all your friends when a guy came around."

Em suddenly remembered the boy who had written his phone number in her cigarette pack. The ink was blurred and indecipherable. "Look at my very important number!" she wailed.

Seated at the diner, Hannah searched her pockets for roaches, carefully emptying them into her napkin. "You call that breakfast?" Em asked.

"When I'm with you, I call it necessary," Hannah replied. Em got up from the table. Donna pumped her fist in the air.

Hannah opened her notebook. She kept notes on their reckless cycles, her aimless conversations with welfare babies. She turned to a fresh page and wrote "The morning after the night before."

Donna put her feet up on the seat and when Em came out of the bathroom she pushed them off. Hannah chewed thoughtfully on her pen.

"Jay was hitting on so me hard last night," Em said.

"Donna made out with him," Hannah said, and felt a pinch under the table. "ow!"

"I did too," Em said, "but I was drunk." They looked at each other suspiciously. The waitress came by to take their order.

"Whatterya writing now, Hannah?" Donna asked.

"I can't believe you," Em said.

"I'm trying to figure out if it's enough in life just to have a good time," Hannah answered.

"How could you doubt that?" Donna asked.

"I sure miss Lily," Hannah said. "We've become a little lost without her."

"You know I used to go out with Jay," Em said.

Donna brushed the hair from her face and laughed. "In that case, I've been dating him longer than you."

"That guy's a creep," Hannah said. "As far as I'm concerned, you couldn't give him away."

The coffee came and they fought over the last of the cream.

The Story of Hannah & Gritboy

PART ONE

Hannah and Gritboy noticed each other before they ever met. One day Gritboy skateboarded down the street, baseball cap turned backwards, past Hannah, who sat on a box as she moved out of the house she shared with an Elvis-obsessed poet. Gritboy glanced at her briefly as Hannah, stoned, stared back through a monocle she'd found while packing.

Gritboy felt giddy and light-headed as he stopped at the corner. Then he ran, flushed, across the highway, cutting through lanes of traffic. Possibilities hung in the air with the smell of barbecues and freshly cut grass. That girl, Gritboy thought, she's gonna be my girlfriend.

*

Hannah had recently come through a bad strain of men, consisting of her old pot dealer, a neurotic punk, a feeble-minded surfer and to change it up, an Amway salesman who lived with his mother. *Dating is an ugly ritual*, she moaned, *an ugly, archaic ritual*. Her girlfriends grimly agreed. Their nights were spent in bars looking for a good, clean fuck, or at least some decent conversation. When she was twenty-one Hannah had been in love and lived in Paris for a year, but when she stood at the airport waiting for the words to make her stay, she found how love ended. Letters petered out and nothing could be set right during late night phone calls. Everything buckled under lack of faith. Hannah refused to speak the French she learned, said it was the language of heartbreak.

Hannah was happy living in the city, having fun and getting drunk with her girls. Then Gritboy came into Mo'Video when she was working the night shift.

"Can you tell me where the Martial Arts section is?" he asked. She pointed and kept scratching her lottery ticket. She looked up and Gritboy was still standing there.

"Hey," he said, lighting up.

"Hiiiiiii!" she said, though she couldn't quite place how she knew him. "Uhh, you can't smoke here, you know."

Gritboy stared dumbly at the cigarette in his hand. She watched as he put it out on the bottom of his shoe then trotted to the back of the store. A feeling came up through her toes, then shot around her stomach. But she clamped down on this, like Em had told her to. Em said cute boys were usually jerks and to ignore them on principle. Hannah knew she was a bad judge of character, a fact proven by the poor quality of weed she often bought. Despite feeling intrigued when Gritboy plopped down two Sonny Cheba movies (she was impressed he rented *Dragon Princess*) and *Eraserhead*, she remained cool. But he seemed friendly and nice, and the length of his eyelashes startled her.

"I met a boy today," she announced to Em as she plopped down on her couch after work and lit a spliff. "Well, I only *kinda* met him, but he's definitely on the list. Definitely." The list consisted of the boy who worked at Benny's Bagels, a mysterious goth who popped up once or twice on Industrial night, and the professor of the Russian Cinema class she took every Thursday.

"Really?" Em asked, immediately perking up. "Tell me!"

"Cute. I dunno, your height, boy hair, goatee, sideburns, pirate hoop. He's a little skate brat but I haven't seen him around. I'd like to borrow those eyelashes for the rest of my life. Cee-rist," she passed the joint to Em who greedily inhaled. "I'm flailing. I don't even know his name."

Em went into a long-winded reverie about boys who'd treated her badly. "Save yourself the hassle," she said. "Get them young, dumb and full of —" Hannah held up her hand. They had already learned from the tragedy of their mothers, absentee prom dates and fathers.

It would take Gritboy a long time to pay for the crimes of his gender.

*

By his very nature (scotch-drinking, skateboard-riding, Slayer-lovin, good-natured and oddly lovable) Gritboy was defined as one of the dirty boys who tortured the streets of the city, but his dealings were honest and precise. He had sisters and knew the hours women spent collectively self-conscious and unhappy in their skin. He had been a high school hippie and retained a certain sensitivity he denied. He never faked amnesia or threw away phone numbers.

A week after the video store encounter, Gritboy went to Club Zero with his friend Jake. Jake lived in a state of perpetual droopiness, tormenting himself with obsessive infatuations. His facial hair changed as often as the women he pursued, and he wrote tragic drinking stories.

"Goddamn it!" he moaned. Gritboy could barely hear over the music. "Sarah has reached into my heart and mangled it with her petty claws."

"Which one is Sarah?" Gritboy asked.

"*Sarah*! Sarah! The girl I met at the Foodfair. God, those eyes ..." Jake clutched himself then began to pick his teeth.

Gritboy turned away and scanned the bar. Last week it had been Sonja, the girl from the English Toffee shop. Suddenly he spotted the girl from the video store standing in the line-up and looking at him. He gave a casual wave and she suddenly became engrossed in the sleeve of her ripped shirt. Her strange hair hung in front of her face and she twisted it behind her ears. Gritboy thought he saw her blush; he found this endearing.

It was White Trash night at Club Zero. Cheap plastic lights covered the mirrors, and the bathroom doors had been replaced by screens.

"I'm home!" Hannah squealed. "Daddy, bring me the corn pone!"

It was the usual crowd: A hotshot she-devil pool mogul smirked at poor shots. An assortment of queens posed at the bar, debating new, young boys and punks in kilts. Groups of middle-aged dykes huddled suspiciously, mingling with their own. Because the club was underground it attracted an eclectic mix and was a good meeting place for all types. Hipsters dotted the room; half the bar was frenzied revellers moving to the dance! dance! dance! hits, and navy men looking unsuccessfully for pickups.

Carrotgirl and Blue were already on their second pitcher. Everyone squeezed in at their table, surreptitiously checking the scene around them. Carrotgirl topped off the mugs, looking green from the case of U-brew she'd polished off at home.

"WAHOO!" she yelled, raising her flexed arm in the air while holding her black granny purse. Her mouth stretched horribly to one side.

"Em, there's that boy I was telling you about," Hannah said excitedly. "Jesus Christ, don't *look*." She covered her face with her shirtsleeves as everyone swivelled their heads.

"He is *such* a cutie," Em agreed.

Jezebel didn't give him much thought. "He looks like a Mama's boy," she denounced.

"Why, cuz he doesn't look like he's just got out of the pokey?"

Em snorted into her glass and almost choked. "He's looking over here, Hannah. He must sense your love pull."

"Hey, that's Gritboy!" Carrotgirl yelled. She frantically waved him over.

"With Jake," Blue groaned. She was forced to remember their squalid, alcoholic affair.

Jake and Gritboy came over, grinning. When introductions were made, Hannah wiped her palm on her jeans before she and Gritboy shook hands. This was followed by an awkward silence. Carrotgirl pretended to eat the lush velour carrot pinned on the lapel of her pantsuit.

"You were supposed to call me when you finished making the beer," Jake said accusingly.

"Don't move," Carrotgirl told Blue drunkenly, adjusting the jester's cap that sat askew on her head. "There."

"Jake, you still owe me, fucker," Blue slurred. "You fleabag. Where's my fucken money?"

Jake launched into a detailed explanation of the importance of free-floating capital in their moneyless subculture. In other words, he didn't have it. Blue scowled across the table.

Carrotgirl and Gritboy knew each other from the old days, when he'd shared an apartment with Blue for three drunken months above a Chinese grocery. "Imagine all of us here," Carrotgirl said. "More *beer!*" They raised a glass to toast themselves in their ragged groupings, the history and forgotten connections that were hard to trace in the city. "WHOO-HOO!" she bellowed. Blue leaned over and belched in Jake's ear.

"We are an incestuous lot," Gritboy agreed.

Hannah nervously tried to think of something to say. "How were the movies?" she asked Gritboy.

"What?"

"*Eraserhead.* The movie. You rented it last week."

"IT'S A METAPHOR FOR IMPURE FEMALE LOVE!" Jake bellowed. Gritboy kicked him under the table.

They all sat and talked for awhile, then Gritboy performed three card tricks and pulled a coin out of Hannah's ear. The two of them went off to play a game of Tetras and everyone at the table began to speculate.

"Hoo-hoo-hoo," Carrotgirl said lasciviously, and put the beer bottle to the O of her lips. Her eyebrows shot up beneath her black bangs.

"She does love that Dickie boy glory," Jezebel said, "and he must like girls with little dirty heads." It was too much for Em, who actually peed her pants laughing. She ran off to the bathroom, and worried all night she smelled.

"Don't take your hands off the wheel," Gritboy said, as Hannah shrieked and waved her arms after missing a line. When they got back to the table, Gritboy asked her about her favourite vegetables. Hannah answered each question from behind her shirtsleeves.

The night was showing promise.

*

Later, they turned on the TV screens, which were broadcasting a variety of cyberporn and acid patterns. Gritboy went to dance and Hannah slipped shakily on the stool beside Carrotgirl, who protectively grabbed the nearest glass of beer.

"Can I borrow just, say, *ten dollars* from you," said Carrotgirl, "and I'll pay you back right tomorrow 'cause I'm going to get some money from my mom. Okay? And then you and I can go out for lunch." Carrotgirl was a bad pony to bet on; everyone knew never to lend her money unless you were prepared to lose it. She would drink it away before the night was over, hit up somebody else, and avoid everyone for days until they forgot.

"So, Gritboy asked me if you had a boyfriend, Hannah." Carrotgirl smiled as Hannah fished a crumpled bill out of her pocket. "He said he thinks you're a hotcake!"

Hannah pretended this news didn't excite her, although it did, and she felt the same old dread. Their entire relationship flashed before her eyes, a rerun of every other coupling. Sharing a drink. Some witty banter. Dropping a few hints, getting drunk and going home together. Hannah pictured herself getting up early and wiping off her makeup. A nervous morning coffee and cigarette. Then if they still liked each other, hoping to see him again and waiting for him to fuck up. How long it took just to be able to call without an excuse. She nervously played with the silver rings on her fingers.

It all seemed like too much to hope for.

*

They had such a good time Hannah asked Gritboy if he wanted to come over and smoke some pot. This was her favourite post-bar activity, she explained. She also sold a little dope on the side for extra cash, which she didn't mention. Everyone else declined her offer to join them; Carrotgirl never smoked up, she was already too weird. Em and Jezebel said they were tired, each giving her a wink. Blue and Jake were still arguing. It was quite clear they would be going home together.

All Gritboy remembered from that night sitting at Hannah's window was that not a single star appeared, but it was a beautiful sky. He looked at her over the candle, which put a strange light in her eyes. *I can't kiss this girl*, he thought, *she's too good for me*.

Much later, when he told this to Hannah, she smacked her forehead. "You fool," she said. "Couldn't you *tell*?"

They sat and told stoner stories. Gritboy described his tyrannical father and his old hippie days and Hannah, self-consciously, told him about a dog movie that had made her cry. Hannah said finding religion was akin to catching a virus, and Gritboy explained the nature of cults. When Hannah got up to make Kool-Aid, she realized they had been talking for hours. Just then Em yelled from next door, "Shut the FUG UP, it's three in the FUGGIN morning!" They shut the window reluctantly.

And years later, one thing could still be extracted from the memory of that night spent together. The moment of wonder when two people fit together, perfectly.

They held on to each other all night.

*

The next morning they woke up shyly. Hannah made coffee while smoking a cigarette. They sat at the kitchen table and looked out the window. Neither one knew what to say. Hannah asked Gritboy if he had plans for the day and he said nah, he definitely didn't.

"It's beautiful outside," she said. "You wanna go on a mushroom trip?" She kept chocolates in the freezer for unplanned occasions.

Gritboy thought for a moment. "Hell, yeah!" He had given up psychedelics some time ago, but he wanted to take a trip that was theirs alone. She packed the supplies and they walked up the highway, putting out their thumbs. A wild-eyed hippie in a pristine Thunderbird picked them up and fed them oranges. They went to a beach up the coast and it seemed faraway, like a distant land. They sat on the sand and talked of moon crickets and sand fleas glowing blue. It was a day like no other, hot and sultry, colours exploding around them. They climbed magical moss-covered trees. After lunch they skipped stones and Hannah fell in the water. Moments expanded to infinity as they searched for a perfect blade of grass. They lay on their stomachs and laughed at the size of their pupils. Walking down the road back to town they wondered how they looked to passing cars, a dreadlocked girl and a dirty, smiling boy. When they got to Hannah's door she knew if he came inside it would be for a long, long time.

*

Hannah had a generally timid nature and hid behind cupped palms to peek at the world. She also stayed very stoned, and sometimes this made her paranoid. She imagined pieces of people that no one else could see, and just as often they didn't exist. A feeling of desperation and loss often struck her at peculiar times: easing into a raspberry-scented bath, doing her laundry or looking through photo albums. She saw the people around her as if they were in a 5x7 Sears portrait, a family captured in a moment and easily lost.

So Hannah pecked at the blurry keys of her typewriter in the half-dead mornings. Sometimes the troubles and sorrows and beauty of her friends, like works in progress under flickering nightclub lights, could make her weep. She gingerly showed onlookers the corners of crumpled, pizza-stained pages.

For as long as Hannah could remember, there had been the sadness inside her. She couldn't assuage the fear that her time with Gritboy was temporary. She worried he'd be hit by a car while skateboarding over to her place late at night. She would lie in bed trying to sleep, convinced he wouldn't come over, that he had met another girl or had suddenly realized she was ugly or uninteresting, that the qualities he found attractive in her weren't really there at all.

"Why is it you never invite me to your place?" she finally asked. "I'm not trying to be nosy, but you've been coming over for awhile. You got something going on the side?" She crouched over the bong on the coffee table, lighter poised.

Gritboy laughed and shook his head. "Hannah, you smoke way too much pot."

"Sorry, what was your answer?"

"Yeah, I do, and the old bitch won't let me bring my girlfriends home!" Hannah didn't even crack a smile. Gritboy sat up. "Okay then," he said, "I'm a drunk and I live in squalor."

Hannah knew Gritboy loved to drink and she wasn't sure if she was far from poverty herself. "I'm a dope dealer and we *dig* squalor, baby," she said.

"I live in an automobile."

"Whaaaat?"

"It's a van," he said quickly. "I'm in between places. It's cool, it's right by the beach."

Hannah relaxed. It seemed like a very romantic notion. "What about winter?"

Gritboy grinned sheepishly. "I haven't encountered that yet."

He explained how he'd bought the van after his roommate, a long-haired and delusional chem student who practised Tai Chi and back-flips in his bedroom, had taken his bedroll and moved to an organic vegetable farm. Gritboy had been left with back rent and a bag of rice. He invited her over to eat some that night. "It's kind of like camping out," he said. "Only you never go home."

At the designated time she banged on the side door of his van, a huge white Chevy parked innocently on a deserted stretch by the beach. Gritboy poked his head out. "Any trouble finding the place?"

"It's the only vehicle in the parking lot."

Hannah was impressed. The van was fully equipped: stereo, stove, fridge, bed. Gritboy handed her a beer and fixed the Christmas lights. "It's not really ready to run, but I'm working on her."

"All the functions of a hedonistic nomad," she said, looking around appreciatively.

"You're a rad girl," he said. "Most people just think I'm a deadbeat." He grabbed her for a kiss, licked her chin and nibbled her ears. Hannah was amazed that everything felt so easy. Already her life before Gritboy was colourless and vague.

"Do you know how to make rice?"

"Wanna get drunk instead?"

*

When Gritboy had first begun to come over, Hannah would glare at him suspiciously, ask strange, leading questions, investigate harmless relationships he had. Then, just as suddenly, she would throw her arms around him as he stood at the stove boiling water for tea, and cover his neck in tiny, soft kisses.

Gritboy and Hannah could spend hours together and never run out of things to talk about. They would go down to the water and Gritboy practised card tricks while Hannah wrote in her notebook. They got stoned and watched alien-conspiracy movies, then went to the roof with a sleeping bag to watch the sky. Sometimes they stayed all day in their pyjamas. She showed him how to find books in the public library and he rescued her plants from their point of near extinction. Gritboy broke his thumb riding and Hannah made him chicken soup even though she didn't eat meat. He brought her oranges. They hung outside of concerts, hustling weed and mocking the band. Gritboy tormented customers while waiting for Hannah at the video store.

When Hannah slept alone she double bolted the door and was glad the cat was there to explain unknown noises. Now she woke up with a strange happiness, a hidden optimism, and sat drinking tea or hot chocolate at the window, holding off on the first cigarette as long as she could. Her head was remarkably clear some mornings, until she made a list of pros and cons of believing in fate. Hannah, everyone said, Hannah, you think too much.

One night Hannah lay fidgeting in bed. She had been quiet and moody all day.

"What's wrong, Hannah?"

"Nothing."

"What's wrong, Hannah?"

"*Nuth*-ing."

"What's wrong, Hannah?"

"Nothing!" A little while later she rolled over. "It's just that ... what if this doesn't last? And I mean, what does?"

"That's the stupidest thing I ever heard," Gritboy said furiously. He fumbled for a cigarette. "You can't think like that!"

Hannah pulled the blanket up to her chin and watched him with wide, brown eyes. Gritboy softened.

"It's too late, you big doughnut. I've already decided." He puffed his cigarette and pulled her close. "If it makes you feel better, I promise I'll never hurt you. And when I lie, my ears turn red." Hannah checked. They were a perfectly natural colour.

The next morning Gritboy jumped up and down on Hannah's bed as she scribbled in her journal. "Make me famous," he squealed.

"Shut up!" She sprawled on her stomach in her skivvies, kicking at him with her back leg. The codeine for his broken thumb had worn off and she knew if he got his hands on some dope he would begin to talk conspiracy theories and the evils of corporate culture.

"Have you got the SPATULA?" Em said, suddenly storming in from next door. "There's a boy I can't get rid of in MY KITCHEN, wearing a pair of MY JEANS," she paused, "and they look better on HIM!"

She strode to the kitchen, where they heard the rattle of pots in the sink. "What happened to THIS?" she said, stomping back in the room waving a mutilated, half-melted spatula.

"I didn't do it!" Hannah said defensively.

"Scramble through the *Stoner's Handbook* lodged in the back of your brain," Gritboy said. "Remember Rule one, Hannah? Do not operate gas stoves if high."

"I may have violated that," she said. "Sorry, Em."

"Christ," Em complained. "It's like the time you and Jezebel tried to fry up some marbles."

"That *was* a bad idea," Hannah admitted. Gritboy rolled across the bed, laughing.

Em threw open the door. "GODDAMN. Do you two always have to be so loud and fucking HAPPY?" Hannah told Gritboy they would have to try and keep it down.

*

The first time Gritboy told Hannah he loved her, they were lying in bed in the late hours. The apartment smelled like rain. Hannah traced circles on the back of his neck and it was a lovely feeling. He let out a half sigh and she reached over and kissed his cheek.

"How did I get an angel girl?" he whispered.

"I'm so lucky," she whispered back.

"No, crazy boys are a dime a dozen, but angel girls are hard to come by."

Water dripped into the plastic bucket on the radiator, as steady as a heartbeat.

PART TWO

Gritboy moved in. After months of sleeping at Hannah's, making lunches and pooling resources for elaborate dinners, losing smelly balls of socks under the bed and watching her shave her legs, he sold his van and gave half the money for rent. It relieved Hannah she no longer had to worry he would be carjacked. Gritboy's van was cozy with the portable heater and star-covered windows, but it didn't have a bathroom, and she hated waking up with yellow, waxy stuffing in her hair from ripped upholstery.

They fell into patterns. They got up and made food and made the bed and went out and came home and got groceries and got drunk and went to bed. In between this they tried to do the dishes and see their old friends. It became a routine so quickly sometimes Hannah wondered if they were waiting for something that wasn't happening and didn't even know it.

"Is this all there is?" she asked once.

Gritboy thought for a moment. "An expectation is defined as something never achieved."

*

It seemed as if they were happy for a long time. Then one day Hannah woke up exhausted. She shifted through dirty clothing, late for work, bellowing, "Fuck fuck FUCK!" Gritboy rolled over and put his head under a pillow. She tried to find food in the demolished kitchen of their post-bar argument and late night snack of mishmash burritos. *I'm twenty-four, I can't believe I'm this tired*, she thought. She popped one of Gritboy's old codeine tablets and grumbled in the bathroom.

Gritboy had no job and even less interest in finding one. He got a welfare cheque each month and promptly drank it away, but while he had money he was full of treats and thoughtful gifts. He didn't ask for much, was content to spend his days reading and skateboarding in the same dirty pants.

Everyone knew Gritboy was a drunk, a fact he cheerfully admitted. Often he stumbled in late, pronouncing each word slowly so not to give away the slur. Eyes blurry and brows furrowed black, he would mutter incoherently and pound the pillows with his fist. But most of the time Gritboy was quiet, easily hurt. He was trying not to drink so much.

*

Hannah sat disgruntled at her typewriter after Gritboy left for a day of skateboarding, and startled herself by barfing on her desk. She was fine after that and on the way to work she spotted Donna across the street, gazing belligerently at passing buses.

"You have to take care of yourself," Donna said, after asking Hannah how she was doing. Hannah's lack of enthusiasm said everything.

"The thing is," Hannah said, and it felt like her stomach was lined with lead, "I'm too young to be a mother."

Gritboy had been lying around for months. Hannah worked all day at Mo'Video to come home and find the bed unmade, the dishes unwashed. Gritboy would be bored and sullen; she'd buy him beer and tried to think of ways he could be entertained. She'd make them food and become irate when he'd tell her he hadn't eaten all day. He was broke, he wasn't practising magic, he was the unemployed house-husband from hell. "I'm not being a drama queen," Hannah said to Donna, "but sometimes I have an irrational feeling our relationship is doomed."

"You don't know why?" Donna demanded.

"Yeah, I guess. I mean, yeah. I feel like I'm putting everything on hold to make him happy. But then, most of the time I don't mind."

"Dump them," Donna advised. "Always. Unless you really are happy," she said thoughtfully, "and stupid enough to let it slip away."

Hannah was relieved when her bus finally came. She looked around, noticing the passengers who looked tired and lonely, and vowed not to be like them. She decided to make a nice dinner for Gritboy when she got home from work, even if he hadn't thought to do the dishes.

*

Gritboy began to suspect that something was up with Hannah. Never the most hygienic girl, she had begun to clean like a madwoman. It was disconcerting to see her organizing the laundry into piles, making strange bean loafs, encouraging him to go and play with his friends. She bought him a bottle of Blue Nun one night, even though she knew wine made him crazy. He would catch her looking at him at the oddest times, staring like he was an exhibit. "What are you looking at?" he'd ask, and she'd shake her head and go back to her book or mixing bowl.

She came home from work one day and deposited two kung fu movies on the VCR. "Thanks," Gritboy said, barely glancing up from his disassembled skateboard on the coffee table.

"Whaddya wanna do?" she asked, jumping on the couch and giving him a kiss. "Do you wanna watch movies? Are you hungry? I'm bored. Do you want to go out?"

"I don't know," he said. "Whatever."

Hannah threw up her hands in exasperation. "Please try. Okay? Try. A little bit."

"Whatever," he said, noticing her wince. "Boredom is simply the want of a desire."

"Are you being a prick? When the hell did you become a prick?" she asked suspiciously.

"There's nothing to do, Hannah. I don't know. This city is boring."

"You used to do things, Gritboy," she said, knowing how it sounded. She moved to the kitchen table. "We used to have fun together."

"I *live* with you. I see you all the time. And when did you stop being a self-sufficient girl?"

Prick, she said under her breath, and went to make another casserole.

*

Hannah sat in the coffee shop with Jezebel, ashtray overflowing. Nothing was going right. Gritboy had gone out drinking and hadn't come home the night before. He had stopped kissing her cheek when he thought she was sleeping in the morning. She paid his rent, and he had already drunk his welfare check for the month. It felt like they were trapped and would never go anywhere. When her friends came over to hang out he would hide in the kitchen complaining of their noise and cackles. "How can I love him and be annoyed so much?" she wondered.

"So why the hell are you going out with him still, Hannah?" Jezebel asked.

"Well, for one, his goatee looks like caramel. And he doesn't guffaw. He sits and listens, then kind of quietly chuckles."

"Huh?"

"Because," Hannah said hopelessly, "he's *Gritboy*."

*

Hannah sat at the kitchen table waiting for Gritboy to come home. He walked in and dropped his knapsack on the floor. She made it clear he was not to come near her. "Where'd you go last night?"

"Hey, I'm sorry. I passed out at Jake's."

"Where'd you go before?"

"The Dirty Dollar."

"Who were you drinking with there?"

"Eli was around for a bit. And Jake came later with Bernice."

"Did *she* go back to his place?"

"Yeah, so? Why, what were *you* doing last night?"

"I went up to Carrotgirl's and got stoned with Blue."

"Big surprise."

"What does that mean?"

"Did it ever occur to you, Hannah," Gritboy said, taking off his shoes, "that maybe you smoke too much shit?"

"It's a good thing I do or I would never be able to deal with you."

"Please don't start getting all jealous. Please don't think evil thoughts." He was tired and wondered if any beers remained from the six-pack in the fridge.

"Gritboy," she said angrily, "we are treating each other with contempt."

"Maybe you are. I'm not."

"If you're not happy, *then say it!*" she nearly shrieked. "But it's pretty goddamn obvious, and you're making me miserable, too!"

They launched into a bitter and useless argument about who was more selfish to live with. Hannah left her clothes lying around the apartment and Gritboy never did the dishes. Nobody vacuumed. They didn't have any money. The effort to move together beyond the mundane details of everyday life was becoming exhausting.

They made up and vowed to try harder.

*

Hannah said, "How can we can treat strangers better than people we know?"

"What say we smoke the roach?" Jezebel offered.

Hannah didn't want to talk anymore about Gritboy, and she gratefully lit up. "Someone turn off this station in my head," she moaned, sprawling across Jezebel on the couch.

"Do you like my shirt?"

"It's great!"

It was St. Patrick's Day and Jezebel, uncharacteristically, was wearing a green rugby jersey. "It's Eli's," she noted. "Or rather, it WAS Eli's. Do you know, I have a shirt from every guy I've gone out with?"

"They gave them to you?"

"No, I took 'em."

"At least you got some good ones."

"Hmmpf." Jezebel stretched her legs out over the coffee table. "Yeah, the clothes were better than the relationships."

Everyone is looking for someone, Hannah thought. We go out drinking beer; old people drag their carcasses on Princess cruises; kids drive by their favourite 7-Eleven; lonely people go through surgeries, place ads, watch romantic comedies; queers do the secret shave or dyke spike.

"You know what I think, Jezebel? I think everyone's really lonely, and it's more apparent in some people because they're desperate, more so than others. But why are people lonely? They want to be loved, right? But what if someone loves you, and you *still* feel lonely?"

Jezebel thought for a moment. "Then they're not doing it right."

*

Jezebel took Hannah away to the big city for the weekend. They began by smoking dope on the ferry with Jezebel's old friend Hank, who worked at a methadone clinic. Hannah remembered hitting the first bar, an ex-peeler joint, and then little else. "I'm going to have a good time!" she exclaimed, as if by saying so it would happen. "I'm going to rawk!" Eventually they ended up at a hardcore club, where they lunged at the chain-link fence that surrounded the dance floor and threw paper cups at a hippie dancing in bare feet. At the end of the night Hannah tried, unsuccessfully, to get a free slice at a pizza joint and ended up mooning a bus on the way home.

The next day they did a wake-and-bake and roamed the city. Jezebel took Hannah to a blow-out party, where she smoked so much dope she passed out over the water bong, reviving periodically to down shots of tequila. Hank and Jezebel talked over Hannah's prone body as the party wound down.

"You think she's having a good time this weekend?" Hank asked.

"Not a chance."

Hannah was glad she couldn't phone long distance to see how little it mattered to Gritboy that she was gone.

*

Back in the city, it was rain and wet, empty streets — the kind of storm that hung outside windows, soaked through army jackets and toques in mere minutes. Just get home, get home, Hannah thought, nearly frozen on her hollowness. She'd been wearing the same clothes all weekend, and a well-dressed Indian family moved away from her when she sat next to them on the ferry.

They caught a ride home with some guy Jez knew from school. Hannah pulled out the weed in the car. "What the hell," he said, "I'll have a hoot." Slipping in and out of traffic, smooth. Heater on, Pink Floyd, only a dim view of the cars they passed. Empty cigarette packs on the floor, the good smell of faded leather. Don't drop me off, Hannah thought. I want to ride and ride and ride ...

*

"I stayed over at Bernice's one night when you were gone." The first words Gritboy said. Hannah felt her stomach drop.

"Bernice!" Hannah knew Bernice was Donna's little sisiter, and had heard the stories from Blue; Bernice was a party girl who had a thing for boyfriends who weren't hers. "That," she said, "is disgusting."

"I was drunk," he said. "Nothing happened. I got drunk at the bar and went to her place to drink rum. I slept on the couch. I swear."

Hannah believed him. One thing could be said about Gritboy: he never lied. Still, he knew how much Bernice would bother her.

"Can you do nothing but insult me?"

"What does that mean?"

"It means you are dragging me down. It means you are doing nothing with your life."

"Get lost. You sound like my mother."

"At least she had the experience of bringing you into the world. I can't even get you off the couch."

"You make me sound pretty useless."

Hannah said nothing.

"Is that what you think?"

"I think if I'm going to be with you, then it shouldn't be a waste of my time."

"And you think it is?"

Hannah took a deep breath. She saw his hands tremble. An image of Gritboy and Bernice flashed in her head.

"You. Think. I'm a waste of your time? Answer me!"

Hannah nodded.

"Then why are we together?" Gritboy shouted.

Hannah clenched her fists. "I don't know."

"Then don't bother."

Hannah hid in the bathroom and came out to see him standing in the hallway with his knapsack and skateboard, wearing the wool cap she had given him for his birthday. They stood looking at each other. He was so angry his eyelashes were wet.

"Gritboy ..." she said, before he turned and left. For the first time there was nothing to say, and after the door slammed she tried to get her feet to move after him, but they wouldn't.

*

In the two weeks that followed, Hannah went through alternate periods of mourning and rage, fear that Gritboy would never come back, fear that she had made a terrible mistake with the only one who would ever really love her. She had been Gritboy's girlfriend so intensely she didn't know who she was without him. But mostly she thought about the look on his face when he left. The thought of him roaming the city, hurt and alone because of her, was agonizing.

"If you're not getting enough then get out," Jezebel said, rock hard. She even threw out photos.

Hannah propped her chin on her palms and looked truly miserable. "When does love become co-dependency? And how do you tell?"

"I saw Gritboy the other day," Eli called and said. "He was all fucked up, just trashed, man, drinking wine and going off about how you kicked him out on the street."

"That's not true. Anyway, he managed just fine before I came along."

"Yeah, but once you have something, it's even harder to go back to nothing."

Everyone had a story. Gritboy was seen in the company of adoring twenty year olds; he was hanging out with Bernice, the most notorious bar humper around; he was moving away; he was in bad shape, man. Hannah tortured herself every night wondering where he was sleeping.

Finally she couldn't take it anymore. She rode over to Jake's, who would know where Gritboy was staying. As she pulled up, Gritboy opened the door.

"Hi," he said nonchalantly. She could never read his poker face. Hannah noticed his goatee seemed longer, and he wore a new hoodie.

"I brought you some oranges. And a pomegranate, too."

"Thanks." Gritboy came down the front steps and took the bag. He looked inside as if it contained lewd foreign objects.

"I worried you weren't eating," she said defensively. "I just happened to be in the neighbourhood."

Gritboy said nothing, but continued to stare at Hannah. She had put some orange streaks in her hair, he could see them under the cap (his cap!) she wore backwards. Hannah leaned over her handlebars.

"I said thanks," he said stiffly.

"I've been worried."

"About what?"

"You? Us? Mad cow disease? Look, I just want you to know I think you were taking me for granted."

"It's a hard case to prove, isn't it?"

Hannah's face closed up again. She turned her bike around. "Everyone's right," she said coolly, "we need some time apart."

Gritboy knew the look on her face. Hannah could keep a grudge longer than anyone he knew. "Wait, how have you been?"

"Miserable," she hesitated. "I've been worried about you."

"I'm fine," Gritboy said, but Hannah noticed his thin cheeks, his grass-stained pants.

"I wanted something to change, but not for you to be homeless. Are you staying here at Jake's?"

"Why do you care? You kicked me out."

Hannah shook her head and Gritboy ignored her. "Yes, you did."

Okay, she wanted to say, *I take it back*, but then she thought about everything they'd lost and having to go through all this again.

"I've been staying at Bernice's."

"WhAAAt?" Hannah's face went white.

"She's letting me crash there. I don't have the van anymore, remember?"

"It's been *two* weeks," Hannah sobbed, pushing off on her bike. "*Two weeks!*"

"No Hannah, wait!"

"Fuck youuuuu!" She was already down the street.

"Hannah!" Gritboy yelled at her retreating figure. "Fuck you, too!"

Gritboy felt terrible. He hadn't meant to say that, at all.

*

Gritboy started to drink uncontrollably, running half-mad through the streets. He sometimes walked by Hannah's window on the way home, despite it being blocks from the quickest route, just to see if her light was on.

He could still smell her on his clothes and remembered driving in a borrowed car earlier in the summer, her hand on the back of his neck.

He began drinking even more, spent hours on a stool at the counter of the bar, searched through the crowds for a glimpse of his angel.

*

It was inevitable they would end up in the same bar. Gritboy tapped Hannah on the shoulder one night at Club Zero as she drank with Em. The look on his face took something out of her knees.

"Hey," he said, "I just wanted to let you know I was here. In case you planned to be weird or anything."

"Er, thanks. I'll let you know." They stood looking at each other. She thought how bizarre it was, how he had been the focus of everything in her life and now they acted like polite relatives.

"I went up to Long Beach surfing and, shit, you wouldn't believe it, Jay lent me his board and it was so smooth ..."

Hannah tuned out as he went into a monologue about orgasmic crests, the big momma wave. All she could think about was how cute he looked, his face baby pink, like he'd just shaved. She could almost smell the soapy sweetness of his skin. *Please please please,* Hannah chanted to herself, *gimme a happy ending.* They were facing the door and suddenly Bernice walked in. She came and stood beside Gritboy and the tips of his ears turned red. Bernice looked at Hannah and wiggled her fingers.

"I'm getting another beer," Hannah said, shoving herself off the stool. "See ya." Sure, it would be a happy ending, she thought. Someone else's.

They spent the night pretending not to watch each other across the room. Hannah sat talking to a Swedish existentialist and heard Gritboy laugh at his fingerless black gloves. Gritboy performed magic tricks for an adoring ballerina while Hannah sat flirting with a table of punkasses. Everyone was surprised at this turn of events.

"What's up?" a boy named Bird asked her. He pushed his Buddy Holly glasses up excitedly. "Did you two split?" He motioned to Gritboy dancing with a young malt shop girl.

"Nah, we're doing our own thing is all," she said. She was proud of her new-found maturity.

"But you guys still live together, right?'

"I think he moved out. Besides, true love shouldn't be possessive or confining."

"Do you wanna be confined under my electric blanket tonight?" Bird asked.

"I still love Gritboy," she said, surprised. "You'd be nothing but a pair of boots."

"Okay," he said good-naturedly, "I understand. But you know, at this point it usually keeps going downhill."

She watched a large-breasted girl accost Gritboy in the back bar by the pool tables. I'm going to beat on her, Hannah thought. "You realize, of course, she's hitting on him because he went out with me. She wants to know what all the fuss is about," she told Em. Gritboy looked their way, guiltily.

"You know it, baby. The forbidden fruit."

"*Gross!*" she shrieked, and threw a cigarette at Em, who picked it up and lit it.

"Oh, go *talk* to him. That's what you both want to do."

"Surely you jest."

Gritboy stumbled over. "I'm drunk, take me home." He clung to the edge of the table. "Hannah? Please?"

*

Hannah crept out of the bathroom and crawled in quietly beside Gritboy. He grumbled in his sleep and spooned her, one arm firmly wrapped around her stomach. It was wrong but it was so nice to have him sleeping beside her again.

She turned to look at Gritboy. The kitchen light was still on and she could see his profile perfectly, his features filled in by memory. With his eyes closed his face seemed to puff up slightly, and his mouth all but disappeared into a thin line. Because of this she used to call him Fetus Boy. "I love you, I love you," she whispered, and tickled her nose on his goatee. Gritboy smiled in his sleep.

"Nothing good lasts forever," Hannah said to Oliver the next day, after Gritboy took the rest of his things and left. "But maybe I didn't try hard enough."

"Bullshit!" Oliver said. He and Hannah were sprawled across her bed. He had come over and heard her crying in the bathtub after Gritboy left, and had made her get out and talk to him. The ends of her hair were still dripping. "Honey, you wanted him to grow and thought you were a reason for him to do that. And you are. That's why he's with Bernice. She has absolutely no expectations for him to live up to." Hannah's stomach dropped and exploded at her feet.

"What are you talking about? What do you mean, he's *with*? He said he sleeps on the couch! Are they *together*?" It was suddenly difficult to form words.

"Hannah, really, what do you think?" Oliver did not believe in cushioning verbs. He laid out the bare facts.

"ALL RIGHT!" Hannah yelled, throwing her body off the bed. "ALRIGHTY THEN! All I ever wanted was for Gritboy to ... The fact that he was losing me wasn't enough to change anything. I never gave up on him, I was just tired of WAITING! Instead, he shacks up with the most notorious WHORE in the goddamn CITY! Is this what you're telling me, Oliver?"

"Yes."

"He never really loved me." It really is true, she thought, dumbfounded. I just didn't matter that much.

*

The phone lines burned up again. Donna was quickly consulted. "Trust me," Donna said. "All they do is sit around and watch TV."

"Fucker," Hannah said. "She's *your* sister."

"*Half*-sister," Donna said. "Why do I gotta keep saying that?"

"He misses you so much, Hannah," Carrotgirl said. "He's so sad. He *loves* you."

Em had to be difficult. "You can't just blame *her.*"

"First Jake and now Gritboy." Blue was amazed. "Bernice really puts the tit back in prostitute."

"Man, didn't Hannah kick him out?" Jake said. "Bird says she tried to take him home last week from the bar."

"I know it hurts, Hannah." Jezebel leaned over and almost patted her shoulder. The incomplete gesture was enough. "This thing with Bernice is temporary. But in that time you will have moved on. He'll have to deal with it sooner or later. And you are better and stronger."

"That's the end of the mourning period," she said, wiping her eyes a final time. She decided anger was much more productive.

*

Gritboy buzzed. "I came to get my Bodem."

Hannah stabbed the button to let him in. He had an inordinate amount of possessions to pick up. "How's Bernice?" she asked bitterly. Gritboy averted his eyes. "Look, I'm just staying there until I move into a new place."

"And fucking her." She turned away and devoted her attention to savagely folding a load of towels. "Don't tell me. I don't want to hear it."

"Bernice knows about you," Gritboy said. "She knows I have no feelings for her."

"Is that all I was? Someone to cook you dinner and wash your socks? A cunt to fuck?"

"The fact that you would even think that," Gritboy said incredulously, "is part of the larger problem."

"What am I supposed to think, being so easily replaced?"

Gritboy secretly enjoyed Hannah's jealousy, as it confirmed she still had feelings for him. He tried not to smile. "You're insane!"

Hannah wanted to slap the smirk on his face. "I'm just fine without you."

The laughter fell from Gritboy instantly.

He walked to the door. "Just remember that, Hannah. You gave up on me first."

*

Gritboy and Bernice sat in the movie theatre. As the lights went down he began to laugh.

"What's so funny?" Bernice asked. She pulled out a pot of lip gloss and began to rub it over and under her lip ring.

"Hannah used to eat oranges all the time. Once she ate an orange at this theater. The movie was really bad and we threw the peels at the usher."

"Hannah," Bernice said bitterly. "I am so sick of hearing about Hannah."

"Get used to it." Gritboy turned back to the screen.

Eventually Bernice did, too.

*

Eli sat on the couch with Hannah. "I'm trying to get stoned the North African way," he said, cupping the bowl with his hands and taking two hoots. "Getting higher with your *mind*." He had come over to expound a new theory he had discovered in the shower.

"The water was hitting me in the chest and that felt really good, ahhhh, and then I moved and the water was hitting me in the face and I couldn't breathe," he motioned raindrops over his face, "and then I moved back and I could think about how the water hitting me felt good again and that's what you have to do," Eli thumped his chest with his thumb, "You have to think from here 'cause that's where everything comes from. If it comes from your head then it gets all fucked up and you rationalize it and think too much and then it's not real. You know?"

"Oh, Eli," she said, "I don't know *anything*."

*

Hannah stood amid the half-filled boxes. There was a quirky methodology to the disarray: boxes of yes, no and maybe. She whirled around the apartment, throwing out old containers of makeup, filing papers, dismantling art projects. The cat jumped on the windowsill and looked at her accusingly. The cat did not like change. He wandered between the boxes, jumping out to attack a dustball or scratch at her ankles.

Everywhere she looked, a piece of Gritboy lingered like an Indian summer. She stacked boxes in the closet. Oliver had agreed to sublet her place, if he could add his own touches, and even promised to talk to the plants every day if she sent postcards. She and Jezebel had bus tickets out of town. "Everywhere I go I see the ghost of Gritboy," she said aloud. "And I am half-sick of shadows, just like the lady of Shallot."

The buzzer rang and she jumped as the door suddenly flung open. Gritboy stood dramatically.

"Hey! Stranger!"

The blood seemed to leave Hannah, then rush back twice as quickly.

"Carrotgirl told me you were leaving," Gritboy said, coming inside.

"For as long as the money lasts," she said, "and it's never enough."

"How did everything happen so fast?" He pulled her off the chair and hugged her until she hugged him back.

"I love you, Hannah. But you have no faith in me."

"I love you, too," she said, pulling away. "That's why I'm leaving." All she could do was hope that when she came back something pure would remain between them. "It feels like I've got to do something but

I don't know what and I can't figure it out if we're together," she said. She bit her lip hard but started crying, again.

Gritboy bummed a cigarette, just like the old days. They sat and smoked in silence.

At the end of the night they crawled into bed together, one last time. "Isn't this where we started?" Gritboy asked. Hannah pulled her arms tighter around him.

They had forgotten so many things.

PART TWO

LEAVING, COMING BACK

The Basement Room

Blue was living in a basement room. The window opened just above ground level, and if she lay on the bed in just the right spot she could watch feet and legs at the bus stop. She imagined the owners of the shoes and matched the pairs of legs into couples. Then she got bored and took a pill from the special candy dish.

The band Gerry Adam's Cousin rented the house, and Blue hated them. Their practice space was right next to her room. The only thing they could play was an old Stones' tune, "A change has come/she's under my thumb." Carrotgirl was dating the singer and had convinced him to let Blue stay downstairs for cheap rent. Carrotgirl made pots of soup for the house. It was the only thing that kept the bass player alive.

Blue had agreed to meet Carrotgirl downtown and decided to walk, even though she'd be late. Sunglasses hid the circles under her eyes and she wore a fake fur jacket and sneakers. She passed a sports bar that hadn't been there a week before. *Fucken city*, she thought. The rowdies in the line-up wore brown loafers and needed neck shaves. "Go to work!" one of them yelled. Blue made an obscene gesture and continued on.

She passed a studio apartment in the artists' ghetto, where she'd spent long hours with a painter. One night they'd dropped acid and gone to the opera; she'd performed on her knees. They'd fucked for hours in his loft until she couldn't tell if she was still high. Suddenly Blue had realized her skin was red and the sheet was rough and scratchy. The mattress was covered in canvas. He'd said, "This will be a beautiful painting." Blue had got out of bed and left him right there.

On the corner she stopped to listen to a guy sing a song about butterfly fish. The drugs were finally kicking in.

*

At the bar, Carrotgirl teetered on a stool, already drunk. She and Blue ordered pints for a few hours and met some people who took them to a swing club. For a while it was sparkles and glitter and gold tequila but then Carrotgirl got too wasted and fell on the dance floor. That's when she broke her nose. She got up and slipped again while the whole room watched. Blood ran into her mouth and still she kept dancing. The bouncer took her out and she clung to the banister, crying. When he threatened to call the cops Blue panicked and gave him Carrotgirl's boyfriend's number. He had a bad temper but she knew he'd calm Carrotgirl down. He came to get Carrotgirl, fists clenched, and told Blue to find her own way home. Carrotgirl screamed, "I HATE YOU!"

Blue went down the block to the bar where her friend Annie worked the door. She stood and swayed drunkenly, and every time someone came in she said, "No charge but you can donate!" then slapped her ass. No one laughed and Annie told her she'd better go home.

Blue staggered down the street and started to sob because the big moon in the sky felt like her only friend. She woke up the next day at noon and even before she registered Carrotgirl's boyfriend yelling upstairs, she knew she'd be leaving. For a minute she felt hopeless and just plain tired, deep in her bones. Then the band started to play that song, and she reached under the bed and grabbed her suitcase. Blue was getting the old feeling again, that it was good to be moving on.

Oliver in the Park

Oliver moved around his new apartment with a scouring pad but the Formica tiles dulled his enthusiasm. He hung his self-portrait, which did not look like him at all but rather like a shifty Lebanese teenager, in the hallway. He moved dustballs from corner to corner, then attempted to unpack his plates and cutlery (all black- and red-handled utensils), and finally collapsed on his couch with an Italian *Vogue*. Oliver wasn't much for keeping house, and Hannah had left it dirty.

He gazed at the wall-sized Morrissey poster hung precisely across from the open window overlooking the street. Morrissey leaned over a large, phallic-shaped hydrant. The poster was a gift from Jezebel. They had met at a benefit opening at the gallery where Em worked, slurping martinis in the corner and talking art trash. Jezebel had left for Montreal with Hannah, and Oliver knew she wouldn't be much for writing letters.

He debated running down the hall in his Peter Pan jammies to see who was awake. It was Saturday morning and he wanted to have coffee and croissants, sit in an outdoor cafe, peruse the bookstores for mysterious men — if only the phone would stop ringing with constant updates. Oliver liked to be at the centre of the scene. It was only noon, however, and he'd wait another half hour before calling Em, who was a monster before her first cup of coffee. Despite his penchant for nightlife, Oliver was an early riser.

Oliver had a knack for organizing fundraisers that, with litres of the house red, turned into elite gatherings under his careful pruning of invitations. He was a necessity for the survival of various non-profit groups and slow dinner parties. His file-o-fax was a wonder in itself, containing the home phone numbers of a Calvin Klein model, flamboyant editors and ambivalent recluse poets. Oliver possessed the unique ability to dress for success, and he thrived in the vicious art world. He found bad manners unspeakably distasteful and had a sharp wit honed for quick defence.

He eventually put on his leopard print shoes and went next door to see if Em wanted to go out for café au lait, his treat. "Hello, it's the crazy slut writer," he said, waltzing into her kitchen. He felt he could do a lot with Em's apartment, and wanted to rip the red chili lights right off the window.

They went to the Milk Bar since it was down the street and Oliver worked there. He liked to make sure things were running smoothly when he wasn't there, but secretly enjoyed it when they weren't.

Ethan served them their coffee. "I just had a table of nasty old bags," he said in his clipped English accent. "How do you deal with them?"

"Easy," Oliver replied, "call them 'gorgeous.'"

"You can get away with that. I can't."

"Ha ha," sang Oliver, "I'm gay and you're not." Ethan was a grad student and Oliver had a crush on him. Oliver still fell in love with straight men. "I'm having a party tonight," he told Ethan, "but only if you're coming."

*

Oliver called for attention. He had a repertoire of party tricks, could twist a dishtowel so it looked like a chicken. His guests sat around his apartment and watched him, Ethan with his friend Michiko, a dainty Japanese harpist. They checked their reflections in the window as they waited to go out. Em came down the hall, having one of her bad days. "I'm beautiful and sexy and charming, so why am I fucking ALONE?"

Oliver rolled his eyes. "That you are, honey pie," he answered, beginning to dance. "Beautiful, that is." He did a sashay. "Enchanté." The Farah Fawcett bust on the bookshelf observed the scene. He concentrated on his technoboy arm movements. He knew about his sexy ass. He manned a sound system of Madonna only.

Ethan was pale and perfect, and Oliver knew he'd keep trying, unsuccessfully, to bed him.

Michiko debated where Em was coming from, and where she would go. She wanted to go down and suck hard. She finished her vodka and cranberry and collected glasses, made new drinks for everyone. Michiko usually didn't play hostess, but she wanted the party to keep going. She plucked at the bottle label with her black fingernails clipped short and painted with precision.

It was early, and the heat and innuendo hung like dull air.

*

After a while, Michiko realized she wouldn't get anywhere with Em. She and Ethan decided to skip the club and watch a foreign film instead. "*No!*" Oliver wailed. "You are poopy," he told Ethan, slightly miffed.

On the walk downtown, Oliver told Em that he wanted to throw Ethan down and come on his face. Oliver felt overweight and unsexy; he complained he needed a new haircut and hated his clothes. He felt like a hausfrau. He wanted desire and didn't even need the sex.

Oliver walked into Club Zero and went to the bathroom to check his appearance. He came out and made a full entrance, decided Em had chosen a suitable location and elaborately dropped his leather coat over one of the high stools. Everyone was getting drunk, already marking potential fucks. Oliver stood beside the table, dancing. He ordered a cranberry juice from Todd, the pouty waiter. Oliver knew everyone's secrets; Todd had a small cock and liked to be called "big Daddy" in bed.

Oliver worked the room for an hour. "I'm *not* going home alone tonight," he informed Em, who scanned the bar.

"What about that guy?" She pointed to a small, stocky man in a tight white shirt. "How about him?"

"Ryan? We call him bowling ball because of all the fingers he likes up his ass!"

"How about him?"

"Oh, you don't want to go there. I got together with him once. That's the guy I told you about, who stuck his dick in the bowl of chocolate pudding in my fridge ..." Oliver had been in the scene too long.

"Oliver, you are so decadent," Em said.

"No, Em, decadence is drinking your own breast milk."

"I know this guy Marcus who you might like, Oliver."

"Why, because he's gay?" Everyone was always trying to set him up with co-workers, their visiting cousin, a friend of a friend's roommate. "I have a bit more criteria." Still, he asked for a description, mulled over the possibilities.

Chris, a waiter at an Indian grill, came to their table. Chris was tall and had one blue eye, one green. "Hey, Oliver," he slurred. "You're looking good tonight."

"Aren't I, though?" Oliver said coyly. Chris loved to flirt. He had grabbed Oliver's ass at the New Year's Eve bash in this same bar.

"Will you dance with me later?" he asked. "I'm sitting right over there."

Oliver nodded and wiggled his fingers. "Kiss kiss," he said. Chris wobbled away.

"What was *that* about?" Em asked. "I didn't know Chris was gay!"

"He's not," Oliver said. "I think he's just confused." He began to dance at the table again then stopped. "I am so sick of being the friendly bi-curious sex toy!"

Em laughed and so did Oliver, but it was tiring for him. Everyone else got to be in love. It didn't seem like much to ask.

*

Oliver left the bar for a quick walk down to the park. He was in the process of crossing over and out of the scene but was still, at times, moved by indefinable fears. As an ex-party boy, Oliver was a member of the pretty boy pastiche, the groups of young, toned men impeccably dressed, who traded partners and poppers with astonishing regularity. Oliver wondered what would happen when they weren't sexy anymore.

"I'm scared to be an old, fat fag," he often said. He needed more than revelry; he wanted love after the lights came on.

At the park he headed down to the hill, where lonely boys sat on benches. He pulled out a pad of paper to write but it was too dark to see the lines.

Eventually, someone came. He was older and wore a London Fog jacket, shiny leather boots. "Do you have the time?" he asked. It was an acceptable beginning.

He smoked silently, and Oliver liked the curve of his jaw in the flattering light. Oliver said he was a poet and this was where he came to write. The man said he lived in a nearby apartment he shared with a lover who had gone to Prague to photograph old buildings. Oliver did not ask about the lover. Why gather unnecessary information?

The man pulled a flask from his pocket, whisky, and it burned Oliver all the way down. It reminded him of his grandfather. *Scotch whisky with a stranger,* Oliver thought, *a good title for a poem.*

Oliver had never fucked someone in the park, though he had been there many times with that purpose in mind. Farther down, closer to the breakers, was the real action: old queens cruising, androgynous angel boys with hairless chests and thin wrists needing a place to sleep, near-naked men standing in circles. But Oliver liked the preamble to sex. He would be embarrassed in the shadows, waiting for his turn.

They drank more scotch. Oliver spoke of his old life when he used to paint. He said he found that in a poem he could explain his fears of losing his looks and being alone. He hoped it translated, did not make him sound vain or pathetic.

The man reached over and touched his face. Oliver was taken with the sureness of the gesture, pushed himself against the man's body, mapping crevices, feeling the folds of material. His fingers were cold, the denim was cold, the zipper was cold metal against his chin.

Oliver kept his eyes open and looked at the sky. There was no moon and he lost track as he tried to count the stars. By the time they pulled apart, Oliver had written a poem.

Bernice

Bernice stood in the middle of the club and swung her long hair once over each shoulder. She had a long, graceful neck that made her look like an exotic bird, and tits she knew could take her anywhere. Her tongue played with the ring in her lip, a black bead in a silver circle.

Bernice had always liked the feeling of closeness with strangers, watching a boy fumble nervously with his cock in an alley. When she was younger she did them for drinks or drugs, or money. She had never understood why they always pulled out and felt so far away, or looked at her as if she were a ghost. Her sisters never told her much. Now she just liked the feeling of power, knowing men wanted to fuck her.

"Play me something I can really move to," Bernice said to the DJ. He eyed her up and down, stopped at her chest, then nodded. On the floor she smiled and shook her body side to side, twirling her arms over her head. She shut her eyes and when she opened them again boys with shiny faces were dancing beside her, just like they always did.

DRINKS FOR THE JADED, JILTED AND SEMI-DELUSIONAL, read the sign above the bar.

The club was about to close and Gritboy hadn't show up. Bernice watched the crowd, how lines were formed, and the idiot messengers in between.

She wanted Gritboy to look at her the way she'd watched him look at Hannah. He said he couldn't help that he still loved his ex-girlfriend. Bernice decided to take home the next boy who talked to her, and it didn't matter what he said because she'd heard it all before. *I can make you see god*, one had whispered, laughably. Smoke and boys' oiliness tasted the same inside her mouth.

*

It was just a few blocks from the bar to his apartment. She held a drink and smoked a cigarette. The boy sprawled across the couch, one hand inside her unbuttoned shirt, his fingers already obscene.

Later, in the taxi on the way home, the driver kept turning around; he was wearing a cheap blue suit and his hair was slicked back over his collar. When Bernice was younger she'd offer to let cabbies feel her up on the way home in exchange for a free ride, but now it was as if sex came from her like a smell, even when she didn't want it. "These irregular buildings inhabit my soul," she said. The driver turned around again and regarded her suspiciously in the rearview mirror.

Gritboy was somewhere in the city, practising magic. He got mad when she called them tricks. *Illusions*, he said, a difference she didn't understand. Gritboy said her life was a combination of self-loathing and shock.

She kept writing the same old story. That's what he'd said once, too.

*

The next night she made Gritboy dinner, wrapped pasta around her tongue, wiggled her ass at the stove. Gritboy told her not to expect anything from him. She said she had written a poem about a boy with a goatee, a boy who didn't really love her. "That's me!" he cried. "Make me famous!" She finally snatched the plates in frustration, threw them in the sink.

They went out and agreed to get drunk. She put her hand on his thigh under the table as he watched a grey-eyed blonde across the room. Bernice told him how she'd fuck them both. She knew Gritboy was watching as she walked toward the mirrors. For once, she was sure of something.

*

The next morning, Bernice was pleased to be lying naked in her bed beside Gritboy. Before last night, he had never even kissed her. After the blonde had got undressed she hadn't stayed long. Bernice had stretched the blonde's naked body across the stained couch and recited a poem about Isis and lavender flowers.

Gritboy woke up, saw Bernice, and flinched away. The blood slowed in the light blue veins traceable on her breasts.

She wondered how long it would take to start over, to be the girl who came first.

Another Dirty Angel

(Some excerpts from Hannah's travel journal):
I don't know if I can survive this broken heart. Gritboy said his memories were like snapshots. The pictures I have are the last days around us like ruins.

Lily tells me I take grace and love with me, even when I feel the least sturdy.

Hannah and Jezebel left the city with a minimum number of socks and T-shirts in their knapsacks. "Only what you want to carry with you," Jezebel warned, and Hannah thought it was a good metaphor all around. Jezebel planned to stay in Montreal. Hannah was going all the way to New York City to visit Blue, who moved there a month ago and already had a job and a place to stay. First they would travel in an arc from San Francisco to Toronto, where they would see Lily, who now lived a few hours away from the city in a small orchard town.

They plotted their invasion, criss-crossing borders: two girls, one tall, one tiny, Jezebel's knife in her pocket and Hannah's hair even wilder, everything they needed on their backs.

*

On the ferry leaving Canada for Seattle, Hannah pulled out her journal. "What are you writing?" Jezebel asked, hoping it wasn't another Gritboy diatribe.

"Drugs and the excursions that go with them," Hannah answered, and as a reward Jezebel showed her the joint she had bought for her from the fisherman downstairs. Hannah said she was glad to be travelling with a Capricorn, a very industrious sign.

They moved to the snack shack and Jezebel bought a foil-wrapped hot dog. Five minutes later she couldn't remember if she had eaten it.

At the till Hannah asked the cashier if she did not agree that having different coloured money made more sense. A greasy man in overalls came in and the cashier yelled, "Homer! Homer!"

Hannah and Jezebel were sure there was nobody named Homer in Canada.

*

Hannah was sick with the pain, and the cold wind of the ferry couldn't empty her head. She knew there were boys besides Gritboy. But even if she did fall in love again, and could convince herself not to dwell on its inevitable end, how long would that take? And why bother, if nothing changed? And how could it, with Gritboy so firmly lodged in her consciousness?

Hannah looked over the railing into the churning water. If she jumped, a year later he'd be in Mexico, some other angel in her place.

destination: anywhere

Hannah stood on the road and ate a peach she'd bought for five cents. On the way to San Francisco they'd decided to save money by hitch-hiking. They put out their thumbs and were picked up by a large woman in an old truck. The cab was filled with chainsaw parts, rotten fruit baskets, oil cans and half-eaten muffins. "I'm Chainsaw Mary," the woman said. Her hands had calluses like a man's. Jezebel sat by the door with her right hand on the handle. Chainsaw Mary told them that she'd graduated from college with a degree, intending to become a high school principal. Her husband left her one day and moved to Guatemala, and she still wondered why. She seemed surprised at the turn her life had taken. Jezebel gave the woman a Camel and she smoked half, then stubbed out the rest on the dash. "To save for later," Chainsaw Mary said, squeezing Hannah's thigh. Jezebel decided they'd pay for bus tickets after all.

twenty-three hours to San Francisco

They eavesdropped on two rockers enthusiastically discussing Peter Frampton and REO Speedwagon. Jezebel was mad because a skinny blonde with scraggly hair took the coveted back seats and there was no chance to get them—she was going all the way to L.A. The bus was filled with cowboys, army cadets complaining of Puerto Ricans, two drunk French men drinking Jack Daniels' and orange juice, old ladies drenched in lavender toilet water, homeboys and bad hair.

Eugene, Redding, Chico, Oroville, so many names they lost track of towns. "Have we hit Weed yet?" Hannah asked, sitting up. "I wanna get a T-shirt!" Sacramento to Oakland the bus was jammed, everyone tired and impatient. Hannah pulled her hat over her eyes and ate codeine. A black woman with red hair sang bits of a hymn and everyone calmed down.

Later Hannah was reading about Greek gods, and she told Jezebel the story of Eros and Psyche. "See, Eros was the god of love and he married Psyche and took her to his castle. But he wouldn't let her see him, he said she wasn't ready. So he would visit her at night, and during the day she roamed around. Then one day she started thinking, maybe this guy is a monster, or maybe he has other wives that he dicks in the day. So one night he's sleeping and she turns on a lamp. And he's the youngest and most beautiful of all the gods. He wakes up and says, 'Okay, I'm actually Love, but I can't live with you because you don't believe in me.' So he left.

"Isn't that the saddest story you ever heard? Jezebel? Ow!"

*

(A letter at the bottom of Hannah's bag):
Hello and goodbye, my dangerous angel. You taught me how to dance at the bottom of these dark lakes.
—*Gritboy*

wicked tiny

"Just a perfect day
you made me forget myself
I thought I was someone else
someone good..."
—Lou Reed, in Hannah's Walkman

Jezebel and Hannah walked to the corner of Haight-Ashbury for a piece of history and found a Ben and Jerry's ice cream parlour across from a tourist shop selling cheap decals and psychedelic flags. They walked around looking for hippies and found drug casualties, coffee bars, tattoo parlours and anarchist bookstores.

"Oi!" Jezebel warned, her code word for oncoming idiot. They were in the park and two boys sat beside them. The boys were from Massachusetts and looking for corruption, or at least an extra cigarette.

"It's yer lucky day," Hannah said to the first one. His friend was tall and gangly and had eyes for Jezebel. "Not the brains of the operation," she whispered to Hannah. They sat together and smoked, four people with nothing in common but a strange city. "Yer wicked tiny, eh?" the boy said to Hannah, smiling, and she was oddly charmed. She imagined they were all hippies and had a free love van driving to Kansas. When they said goodbye at the end of the day Hannah felt wistful. A few days later she had forgotten his name, but not the boy.

*

(On a postcard to Oliver):
WE SAW KEROUAC AVE AND FERLINGHETTI BLVD!

Everywhere Hannah looked, she saw a piece of Gritboy. She couldn't explain it to Jezebel, who would not condone such weakness. Get over it, she'd say, you know you can find another. It wasn't that easy for

Hannah, the signifiers were everywhere—in radio songs, love stories on street marquees. She watched an elderly man tenderly help his wife off the bus and looked away to keep from crying.

She didn't understand how the end of love felt bigger than being in it.

*

Jezebel and Hannah were walking back to their room with the remains of their dinner. A crazy woman with wild hair and eyes jumped from a doorway and hissed, "You packin'?" A cluster of shadows lurked down the street. It sounded like a warning of sorts.

"Yeah, I'm packin' ... potato salad," Jezebel said. The woman was momentarily confused and they took off.

Hannah clapped Jezebel on the back. "Good thing you're Machine Gun Kelly, the baddest blues musician around."

the long dark journey on the bus

(From Hannah's Journal)

Unpainted billboards, the momentum of the bus. Stale piss from the bathroom, a sour odour from the Sacramento businessman rubbing his open thighs toward the girl who looks only eleven. A tired woman with too many kids, trying to get to fucken Milwaukee. The white garbage bags beneath the window hang as useless as our dreams.

"i've traveled over dry earth and floods, hell and high water to bring you my love."

—pj harvey, in Hannah's Walkman

*

"I'm praying for a crash. Or a cigarette break."

"I'm praying this bus is not the afterlife."

A boy named Joe Sarducci peered over the seat and asked if they wanted some honeydew. They had watched Joe talk to nearly every passenger on the bus including a man who looked like he had been seared by acid. The Japanese boy and girl in uncomfortable shoes, a thin girl with badly plucked eyebrows. Two girls in Chelsea cuts Hannah didn't like, for no good reason, and a blonde with an entire square case of makeup beside her. Joe Sarducci told them he lived in Montreal and wrote his number in their book. He asked the bus driver if they could sleep on the luggage rack as Jezebel twisted her body into impossible contortions.

Hannah admired Joe because he was so friendly it transcended gender, race and geography. She thought, maybe I've been wrapped up in myself and Gritboy for too long. Somehow I forgot there was an entire world out there, filled with people. I wanted security from accidents, ridicule, loneliness.

The fabric of so many constructions had worn thin.

*

Hannah's horoscope in The Rock Springs News:
Cancer (June 21-July 22):
 Look beyond the immediate—
Ability to foretell future is honed to razor sharpness.
Travel involved.

(On another postcard to Oliver):
JEZEBEL IS SLEEPING WITH HER MOUTH WIDE OPEN!

*

There is a clear picture in Hannah's mind: the moment the terrible heaviness began to leave her. A bus stop in a small town. She woke and straggled down the steps; it was a hot day in a poor neighbourhood. A group of children in dirt-stained shirts shrieked and played in the street. She squatted and lit a cigarette, smelled oil, gas, and garbage. The people who waited outside were eating fruit, or simply standing, half-asleep on their feet. For a moment Hannah was amazed by the scene: a skinny woman with black roots tenderly holding her baby; two cowboys reminiscing about an old Chico bar; two lonely looking boys in their gangster gear. She was overwhelmed by the thought that they knew what a broken heart felt like, that what separated strangers was so little compared to everything they shared.

That's when it began.

*

They pulled into Toronto late at night. Hannah stayed awake even though her eyes were gritty and sore. She and Jezebel struggled with their packs. After all the concrete, Lily's little cottage sounded like paradise. It was in a small community in the country, near a farmer's market and tiny bookstores. They sat on their packs and smoked a cigarette before they had to move again.

When they found Lily, she threw her arms in the air. She took their packs and rubbed their necks; they drank homemade wine on the porch and watched the rain, dashed back and forth from the hothouse garden with leaves of basil and new tomatoes. At the end of the night they shook off their aches and pains, fell asleep and woke like children in a new, clean world.

*

The purple house beside the river where Lily lived smelled like ylang-ylang, lemon wood oil, cilantro and perfumed candles. Ginger lingered in the corners. Whenever Lily left a place she passed on her plants, and she had trusted Hannah with the care of her favourite jade. Lily was like a hymn they would always remember, and being with her made Hannah see the wonder in the changing colours of leaves. Lily knew it all before her, and it was the way Hannah hoped to go too, on her last, cold days. Hannah learned the dignity in kindness.

(a postcard NOT sent):

I can't forget you, Gritboy. I am drowning in the pools in my mind.

They sat on the porch while Lily cut Hannah's dreadlocks, one by one. While she did, Hannah talked of Gritboy, how their break-up hurt because she'd thought two people made a family. They sat on the porch, listening to the river run. "I know better now," Hannah said, "but I'm worried my memories are corrupting me."

Lily said, "Reach for the pedals."

*

Jezebel and Hannah spent the eight-hour bus ride to Montreal with a thermos of Lily's carrot soup between them. Jezebel began to write a postcard in French. She planned to discover lofts of cultured art students, follow wandering minstrels in black.

They ate at a diner with old velvet wallpaper and walked the cobbled streets. They called Joe Sarducci, who was ecstatic. Hannah rightly assumed he had taken a shine to Jezebel, and promised to do everything in her power to manoeuvre them together. It was Jezebel's trip too, after all.

dance to that, bloody hipster

We went to a club and stood in the screaming music and red lights, and Jezebel said she thought of a gate opening and streams of elves in jesters' clothing pouring out in a whirling Beelzebub procession.
 Jezebel said we're doing the right thing. She said, "Who wants a lifetime of numbness?"

*

Joe and Jezebel decided to fix up Hannah with his friend. Zeke was blind in one eye but a brilliant painter, who Joe said used colour in ways no one had ever seen. On the way home, Hannah shyly held his arm.

"I've never met a punk like you," Zeke said to Hannah as they stood on a plateau above the city to see the lights. He told her that at seventeen a gang of thugs had jumped him. A kick in the face had shattered his glasses and destroyed his eye. He said he walked a fine line. Hannah hesitated and then rubbed his chin with her thumb. "You are so good and sweet," he said.

A moment like that changed a lot.

> *Zeke (the pretty boy)*
> *729-3868*
> *XXOXO*
> *not pollution*
> *fuck pollution*
> *i believe in anarchy*
> *not war*

*

Hannah and Jezebel said goodbye to each other; Jezebel was staying in Montreal, and already Hannah missed her. They stood at the bus depot and shuffled their feet. Jezebel punched Hannah's arm, and Hannah kicked her in return. "See you next Tuesday," Jezebel said, like always, but they both knew she would be gone forever.

Hannah crossed the border again, this time during the eight-hour bus ride on the way to New York City. She woke as the bus arrived in Port Authority. She found a phone booth in the terminal and called Blue. She sat on her knapsack to figure out directions and watched people pass. For the first time, she felt on her own. A black man rubbed her head and blessed her. Crowds pushed by; horns blared, madmen sang. People shouted and laughed with each other. Already Hannah understood anonymity. Being a nobody was the only way to find out who you really were.

Blue was a high-rolling waitress and shared a flat with people who came and went. No one had the room to be solitary. "Find a space," Blue said, and dropped Hannah's bag in the corner. Hannah looked around. A blonde with braids slept something off in the corner. In the kitchen, burnt knives sat on the stove, beside an empty quart of vodka and dried-out limes. The bathroom was slick with oils. A small, dark Swede smoked in the bedroom. There was a dusty mirror on the arm of the couch and a green coat on the floor beside a pair of leather boots Blue said hurt her feet. They drank a bottle of wine and caught up on the times.

Hannah spent the days wandering the city, memorizing maps of neighborhoods. She walked the length of the island, and the width, marvelled at the small space and the huge world that fit inside, the architecture of temples. Hannah felt free of her own memories in the legacies of the runaways and failed artists, icons and doomed lovers who came to this city to hide.

She saw museums and paintings and parks she'd only read about, Times Square at night. The world had been condensed into the brightness of man-made stars. "I've never seen so many lights," Hannah told Blue in amazement. In each crowd, a sidewalk prophet. They befriended bartenders and prostitutes, refugees and drag queens. Hannah learned to move her way through con men and vendors. She partied in hotel rooms with cockroaches and a history, added to the cigarette burns on the carpet.

At a bar she ate mushrooms and drank too many Corona; it was yellow poison in her stomach. The reverend with his kind eyes finished the set and said, "I'll take you home," and then she was riding smooth in a car in Brooklyn at night.

Hannah didn't think about what she missed with Gritboy, but about how much bigger the world had become.

*

Hannah stayed away for a time and then one day she walked through JFK airport in her sunglasses. At the boarding area she set off the detector and was made to empty her pockets. Blue was coming home, too, with a pocket full of money. She said summer in their island city was the best time of year. Blue and Hannah had decided to move in together. Oliver was thrilled that he would get to take over Hannah's apartment permanently, especially since he had finally hung up his shoe tree.

On the plane, Hannah took the window seat. Last chance for epiphany, she thought, settling in.

She wondered what her place would look like. Cat shit and Oliver's cum towels. At least her boxes were already packed. Today, everything sparkled for her, and she carried pretty trinkets for everyone she missed.

The plane hit turbulence and the man across from her gripped his armrest so hard his knuckles were white. Blue was asleep and Hannah turned up her earphones and bounced in the seat, smiling. She looked out the window and it was just clouds, pure and soft, like she could run across them. Nothing scared her much. Anymore.

*

It felt like she'd been a gone a long time, but nothing in the city had changed.

Her apartment was unlocked and Oliver was happy to see her. He gave her soup and cranberry juice, told her about recent injustices, his lost loves and everyone else's.

"You got rid of those smelly dreadlocks," Oliver exclaimed. "Glory be!"

"Where's Gritboy now?" Hannah asked, and smiled to show the fine new wrinkles beside her eyes. "I think I'm ready."

She walked through the rain with Gritboy's new address and it angered her to still feel so much. As if all her experiences were just drops of rain on a windshield, easily wiped away.

Gritboy opened the door and everything rushed over her again. "Hannah!" he cried, and she looked with wonder at the face she'd once loved to exclusion.

She sat on an oversized pillow. It was the same Gritboy space. Stars on the ceiling, plants and pipes, the big fat Buddha at the window. She saw how she would have fit in here, a small table for writing, a pile of crumpled clothes in the corner. Sleeping curled on his mattress by the heater.

She stepped over a purple sweater she assumed was Bernice's, ignored a poem by her feet, written in the flowery script of an innocent. "For Gritboy," it read. Hannah breathed out the pain she felt in her chest. She knew she had pushed Gritboy out into the world, but it was not without love.

He wanted to know everything she'd done, and oddly, Hannah couldn't recall. She remembered Zeke, and the bus rides, wanting to gulp down the country, the salt plateaus, the neon, the misery and street signs. She remembered the pink and purple houses in San Francisco, Joe playing guitar in his kitchen. How New York City had changed her, in the way you can't explain unless you've lived there. That through everything, faces had been kind. None of these things could be put into adequate words. She could forgive Gritboy for living without her. That is what she tried to bring back.

"Hannah," he said, "you cut your hair."

They raised their glasses to old times, again and again, until the last drop from the bottle was like a tiny, perfect tear.

Their story finally ended.

Blue's Tragic Tales

Back in the city, Blue slept on Carrotgirl's couch until the cat began to lose fur. Then for a week she slept in the jam space of the old wooden band house. After a few lucrative drug deals and stolen appliances easily pawned, she and Hannah moved into the top of a red shingled house occupied by two punk bands and a graffiti artist who painted a mural all the way up the front walk. The house was owned by a whore who had become too old to be a hooker and decided to run a flophouse instead.

*

Blue had grown up wild and barefoot. At fifteen she got her diploma on welfare and worked under the table in a restaurant death pit. Her dad was long gone and her mom encouraged independence. One day Blue had got on a bus and just kept travelling. She stopped back in town with stories over the years: the trek to Australia, the tour in Texas with an anarchist band, Mexico with an angel boy who left her with a bag of tattered cloth. She hitchhiked across whole countries and learned how to sleep outdoors well hidden, struggled alone in hard cities like a bit of coloured glass. Sometimes she called her friends late at night and swore this time she was gone for good.

"Home is where you always end up," Blue told Carrotgirl, to explain why she never stayed away for long. Over the years her possessions had slowly diminished. All she owned now was a wooden chessboard and a shelf of shot glasses. What Blue really collected were the stories of strangers.

*

Blue and Carrotgirl shared a bottle of Blue Nun and talked; why Gritboy was still doing card tricks, about the girls Jake dated. Carrotgirl asked why Blue and Jake hadn't stayed together. Blue thought for a long time. "I kept losing the plot," she finally answered.

*

Later, Blue met Jake in a coffee shop. They talked of surfing, lost love, suicide. The middle-aged waitress had a rose tattoo on her ankle under her pantyhose. She wearily poured their third cups of coffee. "The more you want, the more you suffer," Jake said. Blue watched his fingers play with his necklace of charms.

"Are you coming to the party or not?" he asked.

"Yeah," Blue said. "It's time to get high."

At the party Blue watched Jake try to pick up a girl with unruly eyebrows. He resented it when Blue interrupted his conversation to ask for a beer. She sat with her spitefulness in the corner, drained drink after drink, then went home with two cokehead Marxists who talked politics all night and ran out of drugs too early.

The next morning Blue tripped on her baggy pants walking into the restaurant. "Cutie," the waiter said, swinging past. Carrotgirl read the horoscopes solemnly and said her boyfriend had written a song about her falling down drunk in the club and breaking her nose. He was chicken-breast blonde and wore a horseshoe pinkie ring on his left hand.

Carrotgirl had begun to speak to the moon. Blue fiddled with her eyebrow ring and looked around the restaurant. "What kind of a fucking life is this?" she said. Carrotgirl looked quietly out the window. A few more hours until they started drinking for the night. They licked their dry lips.

"Break out the omelette in me," Blue warbled later in the bar. No one, not even Jake, could capture how she burned, the shabby glamour of a drunken diva. How she commanded whole tables with her stories and charming cackles. Hours later she staggered home with a group of boys. They bought drugs in the alley for a mishmash party. Blue forgot she'd ever felt tired.

The next day she woke up in the fading afternoon, spiky-haired and not quite sober. Outside she saw the old hooker sitting on a lawn chair. Her feet rested on the cooler in sparkling red shoes like a middle-aged Dorothy with aching ankles.

Blue stepped onto the balcony. She arranged herself under the umbrella like an absinthe drinker, in repose. "How are you, Mrs. Jones?" she called.

Mrs. Jones lifted her fat arm and waved.

PART THREE:

MOVING ON

Annie & Clay: A History

Hannah: The last time I saw Clay we were sitting around at Em's. Everyone went there to hang out, it was a good place to get messages and pass on the word. I remember Em got really pissy about it, 'cause once Clay and Annie were in your apartment, like sugar ants or junkies, you never got rid of them.

Em: I'm not a drop-in centre for the homeless!

Carrotgirl: Annie was a scooter mama! She was a tough chickie chick with hard knuckles. But she was also a girly-girl. She had a voice like a fraggle. And she was missing her front tooth but she was a really cute girl. It made her dimples really stand out. She was so hung up on Clay. She was always asking "Where's Clay"?

Hannah: Clay, Annie's boyfriend, was this mythical city figure. He had no job and I don't think he had ever actually worked. Him and Annie had no fixed address. He didn't get welfare or any kind of assistance. He was so cute and good-natured, and just so helpless. He'd support his cigarette habit by rolling butts right out of your ashtray. If it was cold you'd find him an extra sweater or a toque. He was completely devoid of material possessions. Clay was a free-floating social program.

Annie: Clay just started wandering off. And then it started getting harder to find him.

Blue: I knew Annie from the old days. She was from a long line of Edmonton punks, y'know the kind who forge through the snow to tear shit up at the strip mall Smitty's. The Farley Mowat thrill. When Annie was fifteen she went out with this guy, Fez, a forty-year-old biker who had been in jail for five years. I heard some bad shit about Annie in those years. I guess her mother came and collected her, all toothless and tattooed, and brought her to the coast.

Annie: I had some rough years and then I moved and tried to get my shit together. I actually tattooed "Trust No Man" across my stomach. Clay was in worse shape than me, though. Carrotgirl would always tell me how weird Clay was, which is funny because she's, like, obsessed with a vegetable. I remember one day I told him I was going to get my hair cut and he said, "You're abandoning me!" Clay really hated to be left alone. I told Carrotgirl this and she said maybe he got nailed to a porch when he was a little kid. But I think if that happens you develop a split personality or something. You don't get upset if someone's getting a trim.

Hannah: You know what he said to me one day after we smoked some dope? "You turned me into a junkie." That guy got so weird when he smoked weed.

A note from Clay's Grandma: Thank you for the birthday card. However, reading it I became very sad. Clay, are you using drugs? If you aren't, please forgive me. If you are, please change.

Gritboy: Clay and I used to skate together. He was really good. I think he just did too many chemicals. That and spray-painting with no mask. He used to bomb everything. Then he just began relaying these bizarre prophecies. Talking about "the Path." Yeah, Clay stopped all chemicals and began to wander, like some kind of mad prophet. I'd wander, too, to get away from Annie. She had this mother thing happening and was always on him about something.

Annie: I was so in love with Clay. He was just like a little kid. If I left Clay lying in bed in the morning and came back that night, he'd be in exactly the same spot. He needed someone to tell him what to do.

Oliver: Hannah was selling pot and people were always hanging out at her place. A very eclectic assortment. At first I thought Clay was just unmotivated. But really, he had no concept of normality. No social skills. He would really try to follow a conversation. And it was hard to understand him because he mumbled. He'd scan your walls almost as if he was looking for secret messages. But everyone liked Clay. He looked like the boy from the Skippy peanut butter commercial. Amazing blue eyes and freckles.

Hannah: Annie and Clay slept around the city on their own story. They were homeless but people put them up. Gritboy let them have his van for a week when he stayed with me. Gritboy had a little cupboard full of vitamins his mom had sent him. I guess she felt bad that her son lived in an automobile. Anyway, Annie and Clay ate them all, ingested this toxic quantity of vitamins. I wouldn't ever let them crash at my place. I heard Clay stayed on someone's couch for six months. And once I walked into my kitchen and Annie had her tongue in the honey pot! I was stoned so at the time it seemed funny.

Carrotgirl: I let them stay over once and they sat on the couch for three days in their long johns, eating candy bars.

Annie: I missed my Portland gang. They all rode scooters and hung out in one certain bar. It's in a secret location. I had just got a job at the largest porn shop in Portland. Clay thought I meant prawns, like in seafood. The store was wild, all these rows of dildos, vibrators, blow-up fat women, cock rings. I wanted the job where you sat downstairs in the video warehouse and when the tags come down you load the movies on a dumb waiter. You can sit around and read or draw. But no, the only openings were to clean the video masturbation room. We needed money; I didn't want to sleep in the park anymore.

Hannah: When Annie was gone, I saw Clay on the street once, pan-handling. It was such a shock, seeing someone you know on a street corner, but more so for Clay because he was really afraid of strangers. I mean, he didn't do too well with people he *knew*. And then to ask them for help. That takes a lot of courage. It's not an easy thing to do.

Gritboy: Clay was over and he was bored. I was upset about some-thing, probably my ex-girlfriend, Hannah. So he goes to the grocery store and comes back with nitrous oxide cartridges, y'know those things for whipped cream containers? And he covers them in a bal-loon and cracks them with a nail. It's the worst high, about thirty sec-onds and you can feel your brain cells being obliterated. Poor man's crack. And Clay goes, laughing, "I've been doing this since I was a lit-tle kid." I think at a really young age he had to start escaping. Bottles of Gravol and beer. A bag of glue at lunchtime. For some kids it's like that. For lots of them.

Em: I used to have a big crush on Clay. The beautiful boy with crazy eyes. He'd come over and just sit cross-legged on the floor for *hours*. When Annie was in Portland, he came over a lot. I thought he liked me so I asked him to spend the night, and he just lay there. I'm like, how can he be in my bed and not touch me? The next morning he expected me to feed and water him!

Hannah: I think Clay poured his soul out in spray cans and that's how he gave to the world. He made the alleys colourful. I was coming home from the bar once and I saw him standing on the street, watching how the moonlight reflected his works of art. It was a way to tell his story. One day all the walls were painted over. Everything he'd said was gone, and I think he just removed himself from a world that took away his voice.

Oliver: I told Clay he intrigued me and I wanted to ask him some questions about his life. I wanted some fodder for a couple of poems I was struggling with. He laughed like I had told him a hilarious joke. Clay was like a foreign species. Life is always stranger than art.

Hannah: We were sitting around and Oliver started grilling Clay. Oliver can be very uncool sometimes, but he just doesn't know. He's like, "So Clay, ever had a fist up your ass?" Then he asked Clay about his father and Clay got really weird. Some stuff...you probably don't want to know. I once had a poetry teacher who told the class to write about the scariest moment from childhood. And I'm like, "Do you really want us to *go* there?" Oliver's from the suburbs and his father's a principal, and his mother is a religious nut who doesn't know her son is gay.

Em: Clay was visiting me and Oliver was there, and I think Hannah. He was in the bathroom for a long time. Then he yells from the bathroom, asking if I had some eyeliner. We're all looking at each other like, "*Now* what?" I tell him where it is and a couple of minutes later he comes out and he's shaved off his eyebrows. *Completely*. But then he had put little stripes over where they should've been, like Frankenstein stitches. He looked like a fucking lunatic but he just sat down and starting talking like everything was normal.

Hannah: After Clay wigged out and left, we started making jokes about a schizophrenic's shopping list: nuts, crackers, cotton batting, Saran Wrap. We really went off about how mental Clay was. I worry that he might have heard us. He had a habit of listening at people's doors. Someone's having a breakdown and what do you do? Smoke a joint and laugh and be thankful it's not you.

Lily: When I was a teenager I volunteered at a free inner-city playschool. There was a boy named Clay, one of those shadow children who never speaks. He peed his pants one day and I took him inside where they kept spare clothing donated by Goodwill. I pulled his pants down and his entire abdomen was an imprint of an iron, still raw. His jeans had been cutting into his skin and he hadn't said a word. *A word.* I took him into the office and gave him a peanut butter sandwich. He thought whole wheat bread was dirty. He just sat on the chair, legs swinging. I remember I went home crying and told my mom I wanted to adopt Clay. When I went back he was gone and they said he was in foster care. I put it out of my mind. It's so easy not to think about things like that. It overwhelms you.

Annie: I came back from Portland to get Clay. I had a nice little place set up. He was supposed to be staying at my mom's but he had taken off. He couldn't deal with family situations. After about two days I found him in the park. It was like he didn't know what was going on. We made it halfway down the block when Clay suddenly banked left and walked into the middle of an empty parking lot. I'm like, "Clay what are you doing?" He was standing still with his head thrown back and his fists opening and closing. I told him to get some help, I was fucking sick of crazies. I got mad and told him I was leaving. Finally I did. I kept looking back and he was still standing and staring at the moon. I walked until I couldn't think of any more reasons to keep going. When I got back Clay was still there, looking up at the sky. Then he yelled, "The moon's gone mad!" and started running. I chased him but he just took off. See, Clay was never really crazy. I guess he just figured that after all the shit he had been through he was supposed to be mental, but it was just an act he pulled. He knew more than he ever let on.

I don't know where he went, but he's been gone a long time. He could be in jail or living on the streets somewhere all fucked up. He could be dead. The worst thing is not knowing. Everyone asks "Where's Clay?" and I tell them I don't know, but I hope he comes home real soon.

Donna Delgado

Donna Delgado's teeth had rotted for years. She sat at a corner table at Wild Bill's Hootenanny, one hand resting on the table and the other covering her mouth. "Get off the stage, you dirt farmer," yelled Bird, the resident heckler, at an accordion-playing comedian. Donna thought of a barefoot man in overalls with three stubby teeth, and what his wife would look like, and pursed her lips together. Singers, poets and drunken banjo players performed each Sunday night at Wild Bill's open mike. Donna lived nearby. Bill was long gone, and the host of these weekly talent shows was a tall, lean woman with a hooked nose who always wore sequined skirts and a cowgirl hat.

Donna saw Hannah looking nervous in the corner and waved her over. Hannah dragged a reluctant Carrotgirl with her.

"I never see you anymore," Hannah said, sitting down.

Donna chewed the end of her pigtail and nodded. "We're like ships passing in the night."

"More like whores passing in the day," Carrotgirl said. She and Donna grinned at each other like monkeys before an attack. No one, not even Donna or Carrotgirl, could remember the source of the animosity between them. Gritboy sat in the corner playing Tetras.

"We ate chocolate-covered mushrooms," Hannah said and quickly ducked her head. "Was that too loud?" she whispered and wiped sweat from her forehead.

Suddenly Carrotgirl covered her eyes. "Oh god, it's the devil!"

Hannah's hair whipped her neck. "Where? What does he look like?"

"There! Wearing a poncho!" Carrotgirl squealed.

"Hannah, don't give her psychedelics," Donna said dryly. "It is completely uninteresting." She made a point of looking at the stage.

A redhead in a cat suit stood at the microphone. The rain had flattened her hair against her cheeks. From her beaded purse she pulled five unevenly folded poems about recent exploits with a misanthropic

Irish physicist who smoked clove cigarettes. The bartender felt her arches ache and turned on the cappuccino machine. The poet shouted over the din of foaming milk.

On her way to get another drink, Donna passed two girls huddled by the lotto machines. "That anarcho was hitting on me! He asked me to go seed bombing with him," one said excitedly.

"What's that?" her friend asked.

"Random pot-planting. Isn't that romantic?"

Donna stood in the drink line-up with a look of carefully constructed boredom. As she looked around, she thought dully of the seven boyfriends she'd had in the past year.

Bird came and stood beside her. "You're looking crazy French," he said as his eyes dropped to her chest. Donna folded her arms and smirked.

"Otto!" Bird yelled at a startled man in a high-waisted suit trying to sneak through the kitchen door. "Trumpet players," he said, and shook his head.

Around Donna, underage girls debated whether or not to show their halter tops. Donna saw Blue, who oddly enough was drinking with a woman in a power suit. She walked over to Blue's table. Blue slammed down her glass. "All I know is, I wouldn't take a four-hour meeting with someone unless we were going to fuck at the end!"

"I don't even have time to meditate," said the suit.

Donna looked around with disgust. "All the men here tonight are dog food."

"I agree," Blue said. "But it would help if I wasn't attracted to unmedicated mental patients."

They quieted down as Oliver, the star poet, began to recite. He hadn't planned to read but had spotted the boy from the bagel shop he wanted to fuck. At the microphone he recited an ode to his foreskin, then a lurid poem about a night spent with a Swedish hockey player. The crowd marvelled at his sculpted sideburns. Someone got up to sing a love song but everyone kept talking. The crowd smiled but seemed more beautiful than they were; it was sad, like an old radio program.

"This is not my idea of a good time," Donna said when Gritboy gave up Tetras and sat down at her now-empty table. They shared a second pitcher. "There're only two cute boys here. And you're not one of them," she added when he spilled his beer. When Hannah and Gritboy had ended their relationship, Gritboy had lived briefly with Donna's half-sister Bernice, for reasons no one understood. Donna watched a young couple in tattoos and purple hair shyly holding hands. "There's nothing like young punks in love," she told Gritboy. "Except, that is, for very old drunks."

Hannah awkwardly navigated her way across the room to their table; Carrotgirl was nowhere to be seen. "I'm so fucked up I just got lost in the bathroom!" Hannah announced. She focused on Gritboy as the light caught the pirate hoop in his ear.

"Oops. I didn't *see* you," she said. "I'm ... leaving!" They marked her progress through the window as she fumbled with the lock on Carrotgirl's red bike. Gritboy rushed outside.

"Come to the Queen Charlottes with me," Bird said to Donna, taking the seat Gritboy had vacated. He was dressed like a gas station attendant, with a name tag on his shirt that read "Lester."

"Why? I don't want to go there. It's cold."

"C'mon, it'll be like *Blue Lagoon*—only overcast!"

"It would never work out between us," Donna told him. "You're not a very nice person." They both found this extremely funny.

"What are you doing after?" Bird asked.

"After *what*?"

Bird wanted to be a player and had no idea how. But he had never said anything about Donna's teeth. She lit a cigarette and exhaled downward. It was depressing to think of her dirty kitchen and colourless TV.

"Donna Delgado and her beautiful sisters," Bird said, and already she could fill in the blanks. She looked at Bird and thought how she would like to tell him about their three different fathers. She wanted to tell him of her mother's grimy bedroom, her late-night phone calls on Seconal and U-brew wine, ashtray perched on the 44DD tits her daughters all had in common. "Get everything you can while you got 'em," was her mother's personal motto. Her mother had a condo full of furniture to prove it. Donna wanted to tell Bird that her youngest sister had quit school, pierced her own eyelid and panhandled, and Bernice used to sit on the laps of her stepfather's middle-aged friends and drink their straight-up rye.

"You wanna know something about my teeth?" she said. "When I was little no one noticed because I never smiled." Bird looked at her blankly.

"I hate my sisters' guts," she said.

"Come over to my place," he said, and put his hand on her knee. "We'll have Popsicles for breakfast."

"Get me another drink," she said and sighed. Outside it rained and rained. In the morning when she woke, it was raining even harder.

Loveless Before Midnight

Donna wanted to leave for the party so she poured Hannah the last of the wine. "Drink up," she ordered. She threw her plastic glass over her shoulder into the sink and turned up the stereo. "PARTY!" Donna pulled up her silver skirt as she danced with the coat rack.

Hannah took a look in the mirror and tipped her bottle morosely.

"Party, party, PARTY," Donna yelled again.

They were going to the annual party at the house on Chambers Street, which meant all types of weirdos were welcome. Clumps of hippies camped in the backyard, punk rockers destroyed furniture, later there would be drunken barbecuing and someone would fall in the pit. The next day everyone would come back to survey the damage. One year a picture had even appeared in a local paper.

Hannah needed to be as oblivious as possible; parties of any kind made her uncomfortable. She always noticed, at some point, that she was the only person not talking to someone. Bailing out of plans with Donna was not an option, if only because Donna would go by herself and constantly torment you with the good time you had missed.

They finished their drinks and left. Down the street, Donna ducked into a corner store for cigarettes. Hannah waited outside with the wilting flowers and newspapers and checked her reflection in the window. A scraggly haired rocker in tight jeans and dirty white sneakers strode by, throwing her a sideways leer. A well-built man of fifty moved determinedly on crutches as his wife followed politely with a wheelchair. Skaters did sidewalk grinds beside the Denny's parking lot as a Turbo Sprint shuddered past blaring dinosaur rock, narrowly missing a malnourished homeboy in a colour-coded track suit, massive phones on his ears droning bitches and money. The streets throbbed with the feel of a Friday night.

Donna ran out of the store, breathless. "Okay, you wanna know punk rock? Punk rock is going into *that* store in *this* neighbourhood at eleven o'clock on a Friday and asking where they keep the tampons." Donna looked slightly unbalanced in her jewelled dog collar and heart-shaped sunglasses — not the kind of girl anyone would mess with. "Care for a nib?" she asked, extending her palm.

A young girl in a backless mini-dress and leather thigh-high boots leaned against a street sign, already looking a hard forty. Her friend jogged around the corner in spiked heels and crimped hair. "Fuck that pole, you bitch!" she shrieked, laughing. "C'mon, fuck it!" The girl turned and gyrated against the metal. A car slowed down in front of them and they straightened their skirts.

The ground blurred and Hannah blinked in the street light, breathing hard. They passed a small, anemic goth in a black cape. White makeup covered his already pale skin. "Hey Gargamel!" Donna laughed. Beside the goth stood a miniature Elvira with a Louise Brooks bob and lip ring, sniffling morosely. "The sphere of the undead!" Donna hollered behind her. "Booga booga!" Red wine hit Donna unnaturally fast. They continued on, taking drinks from the bottles held inside their coats.

They heard the noise from the party at the top of the street. A figure vomited behind the garbage cans in front of the house. "Lookin' good, girl," someone yelled. Hannah made sure her hair was sticking up and followed Donna into the yard. She uncapped the malt liquor and took a long, bitter swallow. "Wait, I'm not prepared," she coughed.

"Remember," Donna said, "no one hits on a girl who sits in the corner and squirms."

"HEEEEYYY, Donna!" Screams echoed off the porch. "HOW YUH DOOON? I HAVEN'T SEEN YAH IN SO LONG, SINCE THE GIG AT MARTY'S HOUSE WHEN WE STOLED THAT VODKA ..."

A German shepherd nuzzled through a mound of empty beer cans. A row of teenage boys in black hooded sweatshirts menacingly lined the front stairs. "You've got the power," one muttered as Hannah pushed past. Another said, "Can I put my cigarette out on your body?" She spat on the grass and the group cheered.

"Let's get debauched!" Donna raised her bottle and pushed into the house through a group of sweaty people. As soon as they were inside, Hannah realized she didn't know a single person. A man played guitar in the corner and a drugged-out hippie girl slumped beside him, singing, "Heeynuh, heyheyhey nuh wahh hey nuhnuhhey heynah." The surrounding crowd laughed.

"Free beer," Donna whispered and made a run for the fridge. Hannah spotted Gritboy's friend Jake at the kitchen table with a group of boys all wearing black gangsta glasses. Jake held the keg in a protective grip.

"Hey!" She had to lean in and scream in his ear. "Is Gritboy here?"

Jake rolled his head back and focused. "Han-nah. He-ey. Uh, I think he's in one of the back rooms." The joint was passed and Jake studied it intently a few inches from his face. "A spicy little number," he said to the boy next to him. "What do you call it?" Hannah squeezed past. "Don't be such a stranger!" he yelled after her.

She worked her way down the gauntlet clogging the hallway. A couple groped each other and moaned. In one of the bedrooms, Gritboy yelled in greeting, his cap jauntily askew on his head. "You came!" he cried. "You've come to make me famous!"

Gritboy introduced Hannah to the group around him and she missed half the names. She made her way to the futon couch, nearly stepping on one of the numerous candles in cans on the floor. She slumped beside Gritboy, ignoring a bleached blonde who glared from his other side. A tanned boy wearing a tea cozy suddenly stopped playing the bongos. "You look like someone I used to know," he said. Hannah shrugged and there was an uncomfortable pause. The bongos continued.

"Have you seen Bernice?" Gritboy asked.

Hannah arranged her features but they resembled not a smile so much as rigor mortis. A wave of jealousy and despair rose in her stomach. Gritboy tried, unsuccessfully, to wink one pink eye.

"Just so you know, you look like one of those albino rabbits," she said.

"I don't think Bernice likes me anymore," he slurred. "And you don't like me, either."

Hannah pushed him away and headed for the door. "And here I thought you were the fucking pirate of love!"

"Come back later," Gritboy called. "Don't miss the seance!"

More people arrived. A giant water bong covered half the coffee table and Hannah listened as a man explained the inner mechanics of the rubber tubes and stoppers. "I'm working on a book," he told her, holding the nozzle to her lips. "It's on political theory." His dirty blond hair fell in his eyes. "It's just my thoughts on really big topics, y'know, religion, toxic waste, hemp products."

"Really?" asked Hannah, gulping her beer. "How far into it are you?"

"Well, I'm going to start it tomorrow. Tomorrow I'm going to write ten pages!"

"Great," said Hannah, looking around. "Well, I should go find my friend."

"Wait, let me tell you about my Jesus home page!"

She pushed her way back to Jake and asked if he had seen Donna. Jake pointed outside. "Don't be such a follower," he yelled. Out on the porch a cluster of people stopped and blandly checked her out.

"It's about REVOLUTION!" a man bellowed, waving a cigarette. He wore a Propagandhi T-shirt and black jeans, with boots that looked freshly oiled. "Knocking out the power lines! Wasting pigs! We have to start taking ACTION, start walking into banks with STICKS, and marching —" Hannah moved away. I'm not into an anarchist diatribe, she thought to tell Donna, I'm just here to get laid.

The teenage boys began smashing beer bottles on the road. Hannah sat on the stairs to watch. A boy with dreadlocks and a filthy sweater squeezed in beside her. "Praise Jah," the boy said, spinning his pipe in a circle and passing it on.

"Good old Jah," Hannah answered, admiring the metal hash pipe. No matter how broke you were, you never got rid of good dope paraphernalia.

A band started playing inside. "The Death Maidens," her porchmate informed her. Hannah felt the bass thump through the walls and feedback penetrated her fogginess; the hash was heavy smoke. "Chick band!" the anarchist screamed, pushing through the crowd and going back into the house.

"You having a good time, little sister?" the boy asked. "Come onnn." He pushed her shoulder lightly. Great, Hannah thought, another slick neo-hippie who wants everyone to share. As if she could tell him that the boy she used to love was right inside that door, a boy who used to wake her in the night to say he dreamed of large brown bears — so many that he walked through a forest and bears hung from trees. A boy who once told her, "My life is hopefulness and hopelessness and bliss."

Hannah realized the dope was kicking in. She wondered whether or not the hippie boy was cute under all that hair. They inched closer together.

Just then a young girl staggered up the steps, crying. "James, oh James," she wailed. The boy grabbed her in a hug and began to murmur softly in her ear. His hands trailed over her shoulders and across her chest. Hannah went silently back inside.

"Watch it," snarled a woman in a tight white tank top as Hannah bumped her way into the kitchen. Trash littered the floor and countertops: lemon rinds, butts in dirty glasses, beer caps. Someone threw a can and the contents splattered against the cabinet.

Everything was grotesque: a woman screeching with laughter as two men tried to lift her top; the crowd jumping up and down in front of the band like a teeming beast; the green-haired bassist drunkenly falling over her amp. Hannah's vision narrowed and she was suddenly convinced she had smoked PCP. She looked around and was seized with the irrational fear it had been spread through the crowd like party dust.

"Oh, the lights look so bright on such a lovely nighttttt," the hippie girl on the couch sang to Hannah. "You're a lonely girl, a lovely, lonely guuuurl ..." Hannah turned and caught the gaze of the man beside her. A thin strand of saliva hung from his bottom lip and his pupils looked like black orbs. "I'm a turnip," he snorted in a thick French accent, "pull me out of the grounnnd."

"Uhhhhh, no, *no*." Hannah moaned and tried to move away. In a panic she twirled and spotted Donna talking to a feather-haired boy. Donna looked immensely bored and this was such a familiar sight that Hannah immediately relaxed. Then she froze again.

Bernice staggered across the kitchen, shaking beer cans to see which were empty. "I can't believe you," Bernice said, coming over to Donna and grabbing her skirt, "plaid is absolutely dead!" Hannah listened and thought how amazed men would be to know the secret jackal nature of many beautiful women. She hid behind two long-haired chemistry students debating Markovnikov Rearrangement in front of the microwave until Bernice left the kitchen. Then she made her way to Donna.

"I really love going to a party with you," Hannah said, pushing herself in. "I can feel this alienated and bored in my own home, y'know."

Donna lazily lit a cigarette with the one she was smoking. Red lipstick greased the filter. "What's with these stinking hippies? Anyway, Carrotgirl was wasted and wanted to take me on, and I just said to Bird, get me outta here so we sat on the back porch and made out."

"Ugh. Where's Carrotgirl?"

"She threw up on the barbecue and Blue took her home."

"I can't believe you left me alone at this party."

"I am an insensitive cunt," Donna agreed. "Hey, there's Franky Sparrow over talking to Bird. I heard he likes you, and he's kind of cute in that big Lenny, farmhand kind of way."

"I wanna go." Hannah stopped her from waving at the boys. "I think I —"

"I don't want to go home yet," Donna said very loudly. Her mouth puckered strangely.

Hannah took a drink. Across the room she watched the boys work their way through a six-pack. They cracked another beer and toasted themselves in the dull glow of the kitchen. The party kept going.

A Girl & Her Father

There was a girl with blonde hair who lived in the city in an apartment she shared with a cat that had never been outside. The cat liked to sit by the window and watch the traffic and when it snowed he would sit on the ledge and try to catch the snowflakes through the glass. The cat also liked to drink beer.

Before the girl came to the city she had lived in a small town where she didn't have blonde hair. She'd been called Emily and had brown, teased hair and wore tight jeans. She'd listened to heavy metal and hot-knifed hash on stovetops, or had sat in the back of pickup trucks on lawn chairs and drunk beer. The girl had gone cruising with her best friends. They'd drunk coffee and complained that there was nothing to do in their small town. They had stood in front of the 7-Eleven a lot, waiting for something to happen.

As soon as she was able, the girl had left the town and gone to the city. Most people stayed in the small town and worked at the mill. The girl's best friend got a job as a checkout girl at the grocery store and bought a Toyota Tercel. Her other friend moved to Calgary and married a mechanic.

The girl liked living in the city and going to different bars and restaurants. She went to coffee shops and movies. She decided to go to school and took art history classes and psychology and learned about painters and Greek gods. She became a vegetarian and tried to take up photography. After class, the girl went to the pub and talked about Buddhism. She talked about feminism and Sartre. The girl liked knowing about existentialism, and even though she didn't have much use for it, she was glad she knew what it meant.

On holidays the girl went home and visited her parents. They still called her Emily sometimes, though she insisted on "Em." Her father liked to hunt and catch fish that her mother would clean and cook for dinner. He thought the girl should be married and keep house. Her mother kept a clean house and even ironed her father's handkerchiefs.

The girl and her mother went shopping together. Her mother bought her socks and underwear and wanted to hear about the boys the girl liked. The girl didn't have much to say. There weren't many boys she particularly liked, and if she did, they weren't around long.

The girl and her father rarely talked. Her father liked to make things in his workshop. He built the girl a set of shelves for her books. He sanded her dresser, removed the chipped white paint and added a coat of varnish. Her father took her combat boots to his workshop and weatherproofed them. The girl didn't like how they smelled and they looked too shiny, but they kept her feet dry.

Every year when the girl came home, her parents seemed a little bit older. Her mother cut her long hair and it became shorter and more grey each visit. She noticed wrinkles on her father's forehead and teased him about the hair that sprouted from his ears. Her father began to go a little deaf and watched TV with the volume full blast. This annoyed the girl and by the end of the week she was glad to go back to the city.

One day the girl got a phone call from her mother. It was fall and the girl wasn't scheduled to come home for many weeks. "Em, your father is not well," her mother said, "and if you can, maybe you should come home." Her mother insisted the girl only come if she could. She said she did not want the girl to miss any classes, since she worked so hard.

When the girl got home, her father was in bed. He had lost a lot of weight and didn't go to the workshop anymore. He stayed in bed and did crossword puzzles and read books about CIA agents and government conspiracies. The girl and her mother watched movies, but the volume on the TV was now low so her mother could listen to her father's movements. Sometimes he would cry out and her mother would get a syringe and bottle from the fridge and go into the bedroom to give her father an injection of morphine. Then her father would be quiet for the rest of the night. In the morning, the girl would go to see her father. "How are you doing?" she would ask. "I'm fine,

Em," he always answered. Then he would wink. She liked it when he winked. It was like he was playing a trick on her.

The girl called her friends back in the city. They told her about parties and DJs, said she should have been there. They sent postcards and letters that said the cat was doing fine and getting fat. The cat missed her and wanted to know when she was coming back.

One day an ambulance came to take her father to the hospital. The girl and her mother moved the bookcase from the hallway to clear a path so the stretcher could go right to the bedroom. The ambulance driver picked up her father and she saw his legs were very thin. His blue pyjamas hung from his hips. She got an extra blanket from the hall closet so he would not get cold in the ambulance. When they wheeled her father out the door, he winked, but the girl did not think the trick was funny anymore.

The girl did not like to visit her father in the hospital. She did not like the green walls and the smell of antiseptic and urine, or the nurses who came in to adjust pillows. The girl did not like the feeding tubes and the bags hanging beneath her father's bed or how he became thinner and his hair fell out. He still did his crossword puzzles, but never finished them. The girl tried when her father dozed off, but she could never get many answers.

The girl sat with her father one day while her mother was in the cafeteria. She thought her father was sleeping and began to read about a town by the Wawanash River. Everyone in the town had a tragic past. It was a good book. Suddenly her father reached out his hand. The girl was startled. "What do you think about this, Em?" he asked.

"About what?" the girl said, even though she knew what he was asking. "What do *you* think about this?" she said, and her father closed his eyes again.

One day, her father moved into a hospital family room that had a couch and a television. One night, the girl was in the room with her mother when her father whimpered. The girl turned on the television so she could not hear him.

The girl went outside and smoked a cigarette. She smoked another and another. Finally she went back inside. She saw two nurses go into her father's room. The girl walked down the hallway slowly. When she opened the door, the curtain around her father's bed was closed. Her mother sat in the chair crying. "Your father is gone," her mother said, and hugged the girl. "Do you want to say goodbye to Daddy?" she asked, but the girl had never called her father Daddy, and she did not want to open the curtain.

The girl ran out of the room and down the hall, past the nurses' station, down the stairs and outside. She sat down on a bench and cried, and while she did she looked up at the sky. She stayed there until her mother came, finally, to get her.

The girl's brother flew home. He was very tall and suntanned. They had not seen each other in a long time. Her brother cried when he hugged her. After that he began to make arrangements. He called the funeral home and the insurance company. The girl's mother made sandwiches and meat trays, arranged pickles and cheeses on platters. Soon relatives began to come. The girl did not want to see them. She had not seen them since she left for the city.

The girl had many uncles, and some of them looked like her father. They smelled like tobacco and whisky and one had a cane while another wore a polyester shirt with the buttons open. They sat quietly and didn't talk very much. They didn't say anything about her bleached hair. They said she had grown up into a nice young lady.

The girl did not like her aunts much. They clucked and fussed around the kitchen. They pulled her mother around and whispered when the girl entered the room. "It's a shame, a shame," they said. They watched her mother with black bird eyes. "What will you ever do?" they asked. Her mother passed them a tray and they picked at crackers.

"What have you done to your hair!" one aunt said to the girl. Her aunt had tightly curled hair a slight shade of blue. The girl wanted to ask her aunt the same thing. Another aunt wanted to know about the classes at university, but the girl didn't speak. She did not want to talk about the city or her friends. She didn't want to talk about her father. The girl sat with her brother and they drank whisky.

After everyone left, the girl's mother took a sleeping pill and her brother passed out from the whiskey. The girl went down to the workshop. It smelled of varnish and sawdust. The girl began talking to her father. She told him about her apartment in the city, and the cat that drank beer. She told him about the boy who'd broken her heart and the pub she liked to sit in after class. She told him everything she knew about French painters. She told her father that the boots he weatherproofed kept her feet exceptionally dry in the rainy city. She asked him why he liked to fish so much. She thought of the bookshelf he'd made for her, how she kept only her very special books on it. The girl realized her father didn't know that, and wondered why she had never told him.

The Last Dogman:

PART TWO

Em reclined across the couch, rubbing the cat absently with her foot. The darkness of her tattoo curved across her hip and she held an unlit cigarette between slightly parted lips. Em had actually begun to think how lighting affected her looks.

There were many things she wanted to do: dance on a beach in clean, sweet air; shatter the boy who never wrote back; start the four-hundred page novel she'd sworn to read; sew the damn flower patch on her jeans.

The buzzer rang. Jay. Everything changed.

Em had been letting Jay come up for over a year, and she still didn't know him any better than the night they'd met. She thought about him endlessly, and uselessly. When he peed at home alone, was the bathroom door open? Did he have a magic word? What did he think about on bus rides and in endless bank machine line-ups? Em had grown up with a much-older brother and tended to over-romanticize boys.

Jay watched talk shows. He rolled. He liked to move it, move it; he was slick with sugar daddy rap. He was monogamous but liked to fuck. Around. He said he was no school, not old school, he was down wid it when you were pissin your diddies, boiy. You talkin' to me? Yah, tough guy. Jay squinted and rubbed his chin thoughtfully; he was one bad motherfucker, he was misunderstood. He was lonely and knew he was a cock. He was scared of girls and their soft secret places. He read Kafka and Camus, too!

It confused Em when she got good lines from horny mini-men, was sent free drinks across the bar. She slept with fiancés, boys who lied about their ages, troubled artists who misspelled her name. The city of tricky boys tried to crack her code and she didn't understand her gaze had more power than the ways it was beaten into submission.

*

Em couldn't recall how it had started with Jay, and it mattered even less: a few close dances and too many beers; a few joints; shared cigarettes. A dull massage that turned into scratches from the cat. The buzzer number and late-night visits. Then the beating of his heart.

Em knew why Jay had come by but she didn't want to fuck. She crossed the room as if she was walking a long gravel road.

Jay put his feet on the coffee table, and waited. Em couldn't think of anything to say, so he laughed crudely. She took a hard pull from her cigarette, desperate for a blow to his machismo. Em believed there was more to Jay than lingo and hipster haircut. She waited for it patiently, looked beneath his catch phrases for meaning, but it was a long time between tender moments. She was exasperated, nervous and wet every time he came by.

Em had seen where Jay lived: boys in menacing clusters who spoke a separate language, who spit on each other and hung out the windows. A living room littered with baseball caps and sex wax, the latest porn, video games, NOFX and old decks.

"Are you going to Bernice's?" she asked him. For some reason, Em was desperate to hold him at the door.

There was a party at Bernice's that night, and Jay said he'd stop by. She watched him skate down the street and thought of troubled, daring boys, all the excuses endured.

*

At the party, a skinny rapper drank too much and passed out cold in the bathtub. Em stood in the hallway and saw Bernice in her room, violently digging through her closet. She stopped when she saw Em watching, and straightened her skirt.

"Is Gritboy coming?" Em asked.

Bernice checked out the window and giggled. "Who knows? I'm waiting for Jay. He's soooo nice."

"Sure," Em snapped, "when he wants to fuck you."

"Do you *think*?"

Downstairs there was laughter, drunk and loud. They went into the living room together and there was Jay, waving a bag of dope. Bernice displayed her pipe in the shape of a large lacquered penis and predictable jokes ensued. The boys hogged the stereo and electrical outlets. Bernice started dancing and all the boys watched. Em clutched her glass and sat in the corner alone. Jay hadn't said a word to her. Bernice walked down the hall and Jay followed. Em was surrounded by boys with dirty fingers and scotch that made her sick. The door of a back room closed and finally she stood up.

*

Hours later, the buzzer rang. Jay.

Em sat on the couch wrapped in an afghan. She let him up because he was so past a line she wondered if he might have something real to say. Em looked good in the light with her face scrubbed like a schoolgirl's, eyes half-lidded with sleep. Jay smelled like beer and snapped his fingers to the music, tried to catch one of her cigarettes in his mouth. "Hey, how do you spell blowjob?" he asked. "One word or two?" Em looked at the clock and he stopped, sat heavily on the couch. Power collected in her palms like planets of her making.

"You know how I am," he said, and it was a perfect sentence of loss.

How Franky Sparrow Fell in Love

Franky Sparrow drove a bottle-green '59 Cadillac Eldorado convertible and had a reputation that preceded him in the city. Everyone knew him; he sold drugs to rock stars and hung out with the roadies. It was a business he'd fallen into by accident because his older brother Jay was a deal maker. Franky was reliable backup because no one ever stiffed him except the girls he liked, who were cute, dirty and usually mean.

"Pull over here," Jay said, and Franky parked in front of an old wooden house. Upstairs, long red curtains blew onto a small balcony. On the sidewalk he pulled up his black hooded sweatshirt and shuffled his sneakers. Jay told him to relax and Franky sighed again. Because of his huge size, closely shaven head and enormous sideburns, as usual his movements were misread.

"Why do I have to come with you?"

Jay cupped his hand to light a cigarette. "You got anything better to do?"

"Is this another blonde in barrettes looking for a cheap dope deal?"

"Look, she buys in bulk, so get to know her," Jay said, and pushed the third doorbell.

"Yah?" yelled a voice.

"Yo, it's Jay and Franky."

"The Dog Breath Brothers." Hannah threw down her keys. "Entray!"

Franky shambled after Jay into a dark hallway that smelled of cheap housing. At the top of the stairs a small girl with brown eyes opened the door. Her hair stuck up in every direction. They came in and she showed them a huge, blossoming bruise over her elbow, then launched into a story about a fight she and Blue had got into at the bar. "It's just like *Barfly*," she said. "We drink and move in wrong directions." She settled onto a pillow beside the coffee table. Kung fu posters hung on purple walls. Chipped knick-knacks and doll heads were crammed on homemade shelves.

"The notorious Franky Sparrow," she said slowly. "You used to skate with Gritboy."

Franky shrugged. "You like kung fu movies?" he asked.

"Gritboy did. I never gave them back."

"He's a good skater."

"That fuck."

Franky looked around for an ashtray and Hannah pushed one across the floor. She told a story of the time she was drunk at Gritboy's sister's wedding and choked on a saltine. Franky knew she used to go out with Gritboy, but she'd disappeared for a while and then Gritboy was with Bernice Delgado. Jay began to roll a joint and Franky took a deep interest in the wall art. Hannah began to explain, with infinite care, the delicacy of wrist bones.

"You fucking trashed Gritboy," Jay said. "You broke his heart."

"If you're going to defend Gritboy, leave and take your henchman with you." Hannah jabbed her cigarette in the air. "I don't want to hear about it, okay? You have no idea about anything you're saying." Franky was silently impressed. "I'll tell you this, though," she said sadly, "that little fucker, he really used to shine."

She ignored Jay while he weighed out the dope, and talked to Franky about books — Dorothy Allison and John Fante. If he believed in astral projection. The meaning of dreams, chick flicks and Preacher comics. Franky argued that comic books and graffiti were the real postmodern artforms. Hannah agreed. He said he would bring over some Hate comics. She said that she had read one issue about thalidomide punk rockers. She said that would be fine.

*

Franky stood in front of Hannah's house a few days later, debating whether or not to ring her doorbell, when something pegged him on the head. He looked at a Hershey's Kiss melting on the sidewalk. He bent down to pick it up and accidentally squashed it under his heel.

Hannah laughed from her balcony. "Hey, Franky! Whad're ya doing?"
"Just fucking the dog," he said, squinting up at the sun. A woman
with a walker made a long arc around him.
"Yeah, I'm not doing much either. Come up and have a smoke!" She
looked like a deranged kewpie doll yelling over the railing. Franky covered his head and lumbered to catch the keys.
"Wassup?" he said inside, taking off his hat. He rubbed his head
nervously.
"Listen, sorry if I was hard on Jay the other day," she said, sitting at
the kitchen table and concentrating on cutting up a large piece of red
construction paper. One strap of her oversize overalls fell off her
shoulder and she pulled it up absently. "I know he's your brother but
he totally plays my friend Em. That guy should not be giving advice to
the lovelorn."
Franky knew she was right. "He's down."
"Yeah, down in the gutter."
"What are you doing?" he asked, motioning to the art supplies
piled on the table.
"Making valentines," she answered. It was almost the end of summer. "Throw me that bag on the coffee table." She rolled a joint and
Franky watched her small knuckles with fascination. "I like to put in
filters," she informed him, "for that special touch." He studied the
magnetic poetry on the fridge and when they finished smoking he
arranged the small bits of plastic into a poem.
"I made you one too," she said. "A valentine." She handed him a picture of a junkyard covered in a pink lipstick kiss. On the bottom it
read, "Meet me in the Dump."
"Cooool," he said. "I like it."
"Yeeeeah. Right on. I like to be crafty." She bent over the table and
applied silver glitter on a glob of white glue. "Dry, dry, dry!" she said,
and touched her finger to it, smearing.
Franky checked out her CDs and played music for a while. "They
always say watch out for the quiet ones," she said suddenly, cutting a

red snowflake. Franky began to make gorilla noises and pulled his ears. Hannah laughed and clutched her stomach. When she stopped, the room grew quiet again. Franky stood and awkwardly cracked his back.

"I guess I should go," he said.

"Why?"

"I don't know," he admitted. She chewed her thumb thoughtfully.

"Wanna smoke a bowl and go to the movies?"

Franky blushed and concentrated on a thread hanging from his ripped shirt sleeve.

"Hey, don't worry, I can treat."

"What movie?"

"I don't know," she said, "who fucken cares?"

"Okay," Franky said and tried to look casual by emitting a tremendous yawn. "But you don't have to pay."

"Yeah, I will. But you can buy the popcorn."

They smoked another joint and went to the theater. When she gave him his ticket she crossed her eyes and stuck out her tongue. He guffawed when people looked at them, she with her strange hair and him with his huge muttonchops. They had decided to see a government conspiracy since they agreed the pot made them paranoid. The only thing Franky was aware of during the movie was the warmth of her knee. When it was over, he walked her to the corner. Hannah kicked at a piece of gum firmly stuck to the sidewalk.

"Okay. Bye!" she trilled, crossing suddenly with the light. Franky felt a strange panic.

"HEY!" he bellowed. "You going to the Chambers Street party?" Hannah turned and walked backwards, raising her palms upward and shrugging. She blew a kiss that momentarily paralyzed him. He had been waiting a long time for something good to happen.

*

Franky huddled for hours by the keg and finally realized she wasn't coming. "Aren't you Franky Sparrow?" asked a skinny redhead with braces. Franky scowled and belched in her direction. The redhead wrinkled her nose and moved away. "This party is lame," he said to his roommate Bird, who squeezed in beside him.

"Tell me about it," Bird said. A cute brunette with a dragon tattoo on her neck walked by and Bird twitched beneath his heart-shaped glasses. Bird had a slight tic that seemed to endear him to girls, although he had recently been dumped by his girlfriend. Franky noticed that Bird had stopped wearing the plastic ring on his wedding finger.

"Idiot," Franky said, and before Bird could respond, Hannah stood in front of them with a six-pack.

"Hey little sister!" Bird said, and gave her a hug.

Franky stood awkwardly. Hannah reached over and punched his arm. "You two know each other?" he asked, looking between them suspiciously.

"Mutual friends," she said. "You guys wanna smoke up?"

"A girl after your own heart, buddy," Bird said, punching him on the other arm, hard.

"Did you just get here?" Franky asked.

"I was in the back, talking to Gritboy," she said, and Franky's heart dropped. She stopped and peered in his face. "Wow," she informed him, "you're totally smashed."

They went onto the balcony with her friend Donna who was drunk and wearing heart- shaped sunglasses, loudly telling jokes about Austrians. Franky liked the way Hannah wore no makeup except for tons of trashy mascara. She had the best sneer he had ever seen. They smoked a joint and Hannah went back in the house. Franky stood on the porch, spitting.

Back inside he found Hannah playing quarters at the table with two bikers. Franky noticed she was smoking a cigar and thought maybe he loved her.

The coin landed in the glass. "Drink!" the bearded biker yelled. He had a long ponytail and homemade blue tattoos across his arms. Hannah picked up the shot glass of tequila.

"Where's the goddamn lime, you fucker!" she roared. Her face was flushed and she hiccuped.

"Two more shots! No swearing!"

She downed the shots and held her belly. "You always pick on the little one," she moaned.

"The littlest one with the most spirit," the grizzled biker said with admiration.

"I'm out," she said. "I just wanted to catch up to Franky." Everyone at the table booed. She came over and stood by Franky, looking around.

"What a fucking waste," she said, and chugged her beer.

Franky nodded and shifted his weight.

"What are you doing?" she asked, and before he could think what to answer Donna and Bird came over with their arms wrapped around each other.

"We're going home to watch a flick," Donna said. "You guys coming?"

"Whaddya watching?"

"*Scarface.*"

"Fuckin' A!" Hannah yelled. "It's, like, my favourite movie!"

They all walked home in the shadows. In the living room, Franky cleared the junk off the table and turned down the lights. Donna and Bird lay down on the couch. It was late but Hannah pulled two beers from her bag. Franky rolled another joint.

"I'm gonna be soooo fucked up," Donna moaned. Hannah took the joint silently. She crawled over to Franky and they leaned against the couch, knees up.

"Do you want a blanket?" Franky asked.

Donna hooted. "Nice move!" Bird yelled, and Franky's face burned. "It's cold."

"Yeah," Hannah smiled. "It is."

Franky tucked himself and Hannah beneath the blanket and it was a little bit of heaven. He hoped the movie would never end. Finally Donna and Bird said they were crashing. Franky and Hannah moved to the vacated couch. They heard the bedroom door close and turned back to the movie.

They sat close and Hannah lit another joint. Franky could feel his hands shaking. When she kissed him it tasted like honey and tequila and he knew he would never get on with his life.

He pulled away when she unzipped her jeans. "Hannah," he said, "the first time I got laid it was only because my brother gave a hippie chick ten hits of acid for free at a beach party." He had no idea what had made him tell her that and swallowed hard.

"I promise I'll never hurt you," she said. "More than you deserve."

A Little Piece of Plague

Carrotgirl concealed a nearly full bottle of rye in her knapsack. She reeled through the crowd in the bar blindly until Em waved her over.

"Come and dance!" Carrotgirl screamed. Her little belly showed slightly between her flowered skirt and Cookie Monster baby tee. Em joined her, swaying her arms. She was in a rare good mood and when she rolled her hips with a naughty smile on her face she looked like a camp counsellor who'd let the boys cop a feel behind the bushes.

"Whoa, that was CRAZEE," Carrotgirl congratulated Em when the song ended. In her excitement, her drink slipped from her fingers. "Oh noooooo! My rye and Coke," she wailed. Em grabbed Carrotgirl's hand, pulling her through the crowd to the bar.

"My friend just dropped her rye and Coke," she told the thinly bearded bartender.

"Well, that's odd, since I just gave her a Coke," he said, wiping the bar.

"Carrotgirl," she hissed. Just as suddenly, she laughed. "You nut."

"Does that mean I hafta buy anudder?" asked Carrotgirl innocently.

"Yes."

"Oh. Okay." She pulled a handful of coins from her knapsack and Em counted the correct change. "Are we gonna drinky more?" she asked.

Em laughed. "That's a fifty-cent question if I ever heard one."

＊

Walking home, Carrotgirl staggered and giggled at Em's rumbling tummy. They debated going to an all-night diner and getting a grilled cheese, but decided on ordering pizza. On the corner homeboy and homegirl blankly sized them up. It had taken many hours of practice to be able to win any stare war. A man walked by a Native woman huddled in a doorway and yelled, "SLUT!"

"*What* did he say to you?" Em asked. The woman ignored her. Carrotgirl kept weaving. Six more blocks.

Em and Carrotgirl passed the pool hall pizzeria and a messy ensemble of street urchins and their dogs. Suddenly Gritboy ran out of the pool hall. They barely recognized him — he was carrying an entire raw pizza. Before they could call to him a man came chasing after him. "DROP THAT PIZZA, YOU ASSHOLE!" the man bellowed. The urchins cheered. Gritboy was already halfway down the block, a sweaty blur. Carrotgirl hiccuped with laughter.

Past the pizza joint and the Dirty Dollar. There was a group in front of the doors, still waiting in line, despite the fact it was well past two and the bar was closed. One more try at a pickup, last chance for romance. Em and Carrotgirl ignored the catcalls. A tall guy in Gor-Tex stopped Em, with an unfortunate line: "Do you want to go ice fishing with me?" he asked earnestly. "Tomorrow?"

Em politely declined.

Finally, they turned down their block. Past the church was one street light. It almost seemed peaceful there, without the yelling down the street. Em stopped smiling as two men came into view, lurching down the sidewalk. The ends of her fingers tingled with spider senses. The rest of the street was empty.

"Where are you *ladies* going?" the first man said. His lips were pulled back; his incisors were longer than his other perfect teeth. He wore a baseball cap and had the bland look of a well-fed college boy. His friend was red-faced and overweight.

"Home," Em said, trying to move past, but there wasn't much room.

"Why, what are ya, a couple of dykes?" His breath stank of beer, garlic. Carrotgirl smelled dead things on him.

"Must be," his friend said. "What a couple of dogs."

"Do you have insecurity about the size of your dick?" Em asked. "Is this why you would harass two girls on the street?"

Ball Cap stopped for one dead moment and suddenly roared, pulled his fist back and tried to punch Em in the face. Sound whistled in her ears. He missed when she dodged, but Em fell over and hit the side of her face on the curb. A banging thud of pain swelled in her nose. It travelled up across her forehead around her head, down her shoulders. She lay sprawled on the ground, heaving with fear. Her bare knees scraped cement as she got up.

"You wanna see my dick, Bitch?" Em heard a zipper and then Carrotgirl's shout. Carrotgirl had taken the bottle of rye from her knapsack and her small hands were balled into fists around its neck

"WE GOTTA GO!" the man's fat friend bellowed, beginning to run. "Go! Go!" Ball Cap tried to grab Em, and with all the strength Em could muster she stomped her thick-heeled boot down on his foot. She turned and twisted her foot, harder. Headlights flashed down the street. Carrotgirl jumped in and smashed the bottle against the back of Ball Cap's head. His skin split open in a shower of liquor and glass.

Em grabbed the man's head as he went down and pushed his face into her knee. Em's mouth was full of blood and a howl, it ran over her lips, dripped down her chin and then all she saw, everywhere, was blood. She was like a mad animal, beating his stomach and ribs. A car slowed down and a middle-aged man's face looked out, mouth opening and closing like a fish. Em brought her fist up and down again, again, again. It was everything she hadn't been taught.

*

The next morning Em sat perched on her bed in a hospital gown. At the hospital they had decided to keep her overnight. They were worried she might have a concussion. Her roommate was a monolithic shape snoring underneath a sheet.

"Who's that, Darth Vader?" Carrotgirl whispered.

"I keep listening to make sure she's still breathing," Em whispered back. "I can't wait to get out of here. You can't believe how many times I've heard the words bowel and colostomy since I've been here."

She was waiting for the doctor to come and tell her she could go.

She had a bandage over her nose and it felt like her nasal cavity was filled with rubber cement.

"It's not like we live in fucking Beirut or Northern Ireland," Em said.

"Well, you can't stop walking down the street," Carrotgirl said.

*

Em left the hospital, accompanied to a side door by a nurse who had taken a shine to her trashy magazines and quirky, concerned friends. The nurse was a Vietnamese woman who didn't speak above a whisper, and when she smiled it was so tender it looked like her face was about to shatter into a thousand pieces of delicate crystal. She told Em her daughter was a very good girl who had been pepper-sprayed by policemen at a rave, just for dancing

When Em got home there was a party waiting. Oliver had spent an hour at the Dollar Store looking for a present. He had bought magic rocks for Em, and a finger-painting kit for Carrotgirl. He told them how he had stood at a loss in the aisles. The events of last night made the Dollar Store's coloured balls, Coca-cola phones, rubber chickens, gummy lipstick, paper fans and peacock feather pens seem more ridiculous than usual.

Em was worried about smoking pot with a possible concussion — the flow of blood to her brain. Her friends convinced her it was okay. Hannah climbed right on top of her and gave her a hug like an octopus. "It's too bad this had to happen for you to come and visit," Em said. She was propped up near the demolished remains of Hannah's cake. Donna set up some turntables and Carrotgirl sat in the corner, blowing up balloons between glasses of punch. Eli had brought over three pizza pies, and it felt like a real grown-up party. "They gave me codeine at the hospital!" Em crowed. "I say we *all* get fucked up!" Everyone pooled their dope and they rolled another giant blunt.

Em told the story of last night over and over, and they cheered Carrotgirl every time. "All that rye wasted," Carrotgirl moaned. "After the cops left I wanted to go down and lick the sidewalk."

"Some of the blood's still there," Oliver said. There was an uneasy moment of silence until the buzzer rang.

Em opened the door and there stood Jay, looking nervous and holding a big box of chocolates. "Hey Punchy!" he said. "I heard you girls beat some motherfucker down!"

Ah shit, Em thought, here we go again.

The party raged for many hours. Everyone wanted to spread the love they could. Donna gave Carrotgirl a smack on the lips. Jay told Em she looked hot with that band-aid. Oliver drank his bottle of wine and tried to rouse Eli into a game of strip charades. Gritboy brought his Buddha from home and made everyone rub his belly. Hannah and Franky hugged in the kitchen. Oliver put on "I Will Survive" by the BeeGees and began to go-go dance on the coffee table.

"Girls gotta stick together," Carrotgirl said as she and Donna tangoed across the room. Em sat and watched. Her fist hurt like hell.

The Last Days of Carrotgirl

I.

"I'm moving to Portland," said Carrotgirl. She did a kick dance. "It's a good thing my plant is already dying."

"Why go to Portland? It's just as depressing there as it is here."

"Yes," she agreed, tucking her hair behind her ear, "but it's a new depressing."

*

Later, by the window: "I hope I don't get shot in Portland."

"It's like winning the lottery."

"People win the lottery?"

"Yeah, you win the lottery or get the bullet."

*

Carrotgirl lay on the bed like Snow White in exile. Her green taffeta frock covered her knees and her white stocking feet were encased in shiny Mary Janes. Her head rested by the electrical socket and she looked plugged in.

"Carrotgirl, do you want some juice?"

"Would I pass up juice?"

"It's mandarin crystals. And it's warm. Do you still want some?"

"Did you say waffle? I can't pass up waffles."

*

Carrotgirl was moving to Portland with Annie, whose white buzz cut was startling against her rich brown skin, and her eyes so sad and blue.

Annie rode a scooter and dressed like a gas jockey from a fifties service station. Carrotgirl wanted to follow the caravan south, with the warm weather, and wear a blinking beanie cap across the border.

"Mount this, mountie."

"Hey, CaNOOK."

Carrotgirl made friends.

*

Carrotgirl was through with the city, and planned to dye her hair red before she left.

II.

When Carrotgirl disappeared she left unfinished paintings, fake fur coats. A trail of broken hearts. An emptiness downtown.

Some girls know all the bartenders, and one day end up welfare mamas, with two skinny kids and nights at karaoke. But the charm of a Carrotgirl lasts forever. Don't expect to see her, freckled and defeated on the curb.

III.

A blonde gobbled a joint in the corner. Everyone carried their hidden porn. The trees around the church moved delicately in the hot wind, a faint rustle against austere gilt stone. In the room, three flies buzzed in frantic circles around each other.

Later: there was magic to be found. The blonde seemed like an insightful angel. Carrotgirl on the kitchen couch dreamed of buttons, strands of hair, loose threads to be burned.

She had all the glory.

The story unfolds.

IV.

Carrotgirl wore day-of-the-week underwear. In black.

V.

Carrotgirl was never going to work in the doughnut shop. What if she began to buy gourmet licorice? To say Daddy-O and slap strangers on the back? Would she penetrate the corporate power structure? Would they make her eat Spam, spork and the mysterious jelly lubricant? Would she age under a fine sprinkling of powdered sugar, fingers sticky with chocolate, coins and crumbs in the bottom of her apron? Would the bastards grind her down?

All Carrotgirl knew was the shimmer of her silver rain jacket. To never watch television news. How to talk to the aliens on earth. When she did her happy dance she looked like Charlie Chaplin. A bing cherry in a bowl of weakly yellow pineapple, small and sweet and defiant.

"I'm gonna win this race," Carrotgirl said.

Deep down, she burned.

Last Call

"Love," Blue sneered. "I'll show you how to get over a broken heart." She downed her shot and slammed the glass on the counter. "There," she said. "Ready to take out the stitches." And she just about meant it.

*

Blue had once liked a boy with broken teeth. The boy had liked her back. Some nights he slipped away from the pack of roving boys and called up at her window. Her orange walls glowed like a pumpkin. He woke up cheerful every morning and it was something she admired. The boy began to stay longer. He napped on the couch. *The sweet talk don' last long*, Blue said. But somehow, she fell in love.

One morning at the boy's place she sat in her underwear at the kitchen table as he got ready for work. She realized she'd feel sick all day until she saw him again. And he looked bored. When she left, she wanted to slip a note in the mailbox with his key that said *I hate you* but would really mean *all I ever knew of love was how to shoot somebody who outdrew ya*, like Jeff Buckley sang before he drowned one summer in the Mississippi.

She filled her mouth with words like sour pebbles. Found herself snarling. Always at the stove with a plastic bottle and hot knives. *Wha?* She couldn't beat him and it was like a sickness that twisted knots in her hair. She cried. Got drunk and wanted to fuck. Got drunk and clawed at his face. Finally the boy forgot the rainy days in bed and her half-closed eyes.

Once, when she was sick, he had run across a park with her in his arms, heart racing. Blue just couldn't forget that.

(Means I Love You)

Hannah put the knives in the burners and turned on the stove. They were out of pot and coming close to the last cigarette. Soon they would have to take back cans and roll pennies, but not right away. Blue cleaned out her pipe and rolled the resin into small balls of hash. Hannah liked how they passed the rainy days.

They lived in an old house in a bad part of town, clear across the city from the red brick building where Hannah had stayed so long. The kitchen light was broken but they were too scared to complain to the landlady since they'd only paid half the rent. Hannah worked in the best video store in town and Blue had got her a second job at the restaurant where she worked. They smoked weed in the walk-in freezer with Carlos and the other cooks. The months began to blur, but what fun times.

Gritboy was trying to get straight and Blue had said he could stay with them, but they were still drinking beer in the bedroom. They had a lot of nicknames between them. The love Hannah once had for Gritboy seemed long ago, but if they sat in the same room together for too long the air never seemed to settle. Gritboy complained that his back hurt, and he put a lot of shit up his nose.

What Gritboy didn't know was that after it had ended, Hannah had wanted to get *Love* tattooed on her arm so she wouldn't forget that magic. Now she loved Franky and said *I'd pull out a tooth to make sure we stayed together forever.* She peeled at a skull sticker on the fridge while the knives turned red.

Blue came into the kitchen and opened a window. The wind smelled like rain and the city looked like a black sea filled with jewels.

Hannah thought of each light as a person she might meet one day, she thought of Jezebel and Lily and all the people she knew, and for a moment she was astonished that a small girl could have such a big life. Down the hall in the bathroom, her purple dress with orange flowers and flames swung gently from the shower rod, with timing that seemed perfect.

"Blue," she said, "what a beautiful day it's been."

EPILOGUE

THE END OF THE DAY

Carrotgirl wandered the strip mall, choosing between gin/vodka or rye/scotch on alternate days. One day she decided to stop eating soup, then met a nice boy and quit drinking. They have a little cottage together.

Eli married a girl who collects vintage dresses, but he has never forgotten Jezebel.

Oliver dropped from the scene and bought a condo near the beach. He won a prize for a book of poems called *Whisky on a Cold Night with a Stranger.*

Jezebel became a famous sculptor and moved to a penthouse encased in metal. She has a lot of money and feels very safe. She never opens the balcony doors.

Em let the bitterness fill her belly, and her heart, and the empty places in her bones. She held a grudge longer than anyone and planned to have bouncers at her funeral to ask, "What are you doing here? Em never liked you." She keeps a current list.

Bernice fucked her poetry professor and based a career of poems on it.

Hannah developed a powerful strain of marijuana with Franky. She gardens in the morning and practises the French she thought she had forgotten.

Jay moved to Toronto and began dating a stripper with silicone breasts. He told his friends, "It's serious. She's the chick I want to stick my dick into for the rest of my life."

Donna joined the Death Maidens and they became the punk band Squawk.

Annie stopped waiting. Clay never made it home.

Blue now lives with a Hell's Angel and his two kids, who love her very much. She gives them trouble for riding on the bike with no socks.

Gritboy became a famous, tortured drunk. Everyone knows him down on the docks. He likes to submerge in the tub with his plastic dinosaurs. He still has magic on his mind.

Lily took a wooden trunk full of books to a tiny Pacific island. Every morning she sweeps her hut with a palm leaf in a sarong the colour of the sea. She is as brown as a nut. The girls down the beach bring her presents of fruit and coloured shells. "Only when you accept heartache," Lily tells them, "can you truly love."

ACKNOWLEDGEMENTS

This book would not have been written without the help of these people:

My family — Sharon, Chuck, Mike, Heather, Terry, Rachel, Ashley and Kathleen, who gave me their unconditional support.

Shane Book and Brad Cran, who started Smoking Lung Press and during the whisky sessions became my first editors.

Chris Hutchinson, for his honesty, helpful critiques and Gritboy magic.

Richard Van Camp, whose generosity and encouragement are limitless.

And Billeh Nickersen, for his talent, special edits and mothering.

Carolyn Swayze, an extraordinary agent who took a chance on an urchin like me.

Lynn Henry, my editor, whose suggestions and support have been invaluable.

And the whole Raincoast/Polestar crew, for all the work they've done.

A special thanks to Dylan Surridge, for his amazing snaps (www.punkass.ca); Valerya Edelman for her short film "Girls"; Alex C., and B.L.T.

Most of all, I owe this book to Lynn, Colette, Sherry, Anita, Sherry Berry, Michelle, and Tanisha, who were the coolest girls on the block.

ABOUT THE AUTHOR

Dylan Surridge

Teresa McWhirter has spent the last ten years gathering information and experiences to use in her writing. After graduating high school in the East Kootenays of British Columbia, she went to Europe for a year, then returned to Canada to attend the University of Victoria. She received a BA with Distinction in English and Writing and met the founders of Smoking Lung Press, who printed her chapbook. She then taught English in Korea, drifted through Thailand, and traveled across Canada and the USA, sleeping on borrowed couches and working as a nanny, ice-cream truck driver, landscaper and secretary. For the last few years, she has lived in Vancouver's east side. She has published widely with alternative lifestyle and literary magazines like *The Nerve, sub-Terrain, Geist, Bust* and *Vice*.

MORE FINE FICTION FROM POLESTAR AND RAINCOAST

Pool-Hopping and Other Stories • by Anne Fleming
Shortlisted for the Governor-General's Award, the Ethel Wilson Fiction Prize and the Danuta Gleed Award. "Fleming's evenhanded, sharp-eyed and often hilarious narratives traverse the frenzied chaos of urban life with ease and precision." — *The Georgia Straight*
1-896095-18-6 • $16.95 CAN / $13.95 USA

What's Left Us • by Aislinn Hunter
Six stories and an unforgettable novella by a prodigiously talented writer. "Aislinn Hunter is a gifted writer with a fresh energetic voice and a sharp eye for the detail that draws you irresistibly into the intimacies of her story." — Jack Hodgins
1-55192-412-9 • $19.95 CAN / $15.95 USA

Mount Appetite • by Bill Gaston
Astounding stories by a writer whose work is "gentle, humorous, absurd, beautiful, spiritual, dark and sexy. Gaston deserves to dwell in the company of Findley, Atwood and Munro as one of this country's outstanding literary treasures." — *The Globe and Mail*
1-55192-451-X • $19.95 CAN / $15.95 USA

A Reckless Moon and Other Stories • by Dianne Warren
A beautifully written book about human fragility, endorsed by Bonnie Burnard. "Warren is clearly one of a new generation of short-story writers who have learned their craft in the wake of such luminaries as Raymond Carver and Ann Beattie ... Her prose is lucid and precise." —*Books in Canada*
1-55192-455-2 • $19.95 CAN / $15.95 USA

A Sack of Teeth • by Grant Buday
This darkly humorous novel paints an unforgettable portrait of one extraordinary day in the life of a father, a mother and a six-year-old child in September 1965. "Buday's genius is that of the storyteller." — *Vancouver Sun*
1-55192-457-9 • $21.95 CAN / $15.95 USA

Small Accidents • by Andrew Gray
Twelve dazzling stories by a Journey Prize finalist. "Andrew Gray tells tall tales that tap into the hubris of the human condition ...He expertly depicts the gore of human error and conveys a present as startling as a car wreck." — *Hal Niedzviecki*
1-55192-508-7 • $19.95 CAN / $s14.95 USA